THE SANTA CRUZ GURU MURDERS

a mystery by
Marc Darrow

OTTER B BOOKS
Santa Cruz
California

*To Cathy — The
Queen of DBT.
Best Wishes,
Marc Darrow*

Also by Marc Darrow:
SHRINKING THE TRUTH

The Santa Cruz Guru Murders is a paperback original mystery published by OTTER B BOOKS, October 1995. Information concerning rights to reprint this book or portions thereof in any form except as provided by the U.S. copyright law may be obtained by contacting the publisher at 1891-16th Avenue, Santa Cruz, CA 95062; (408) 476-5334.

Second printing, 1997.

Printed by arrangement with the author.

Manufactured in the United States of America.

ISBN 0-9617681-8-5

The cover design is by Lizardgraphics.

To Karma the dog,
who is probably now a goddess, or at least
a rockabilly guitarist.

One

In mid-October, Slocum received the color postcard of a two-headed pig. The pig wore two different hats. On the left head was a straw cowboy hat; on the right was a black top hat. The pig did not appear to be happy about the situation. Whether it was the hats, the extra head, or the inconvenience of the photography session wasn't clear. He looked pissed enough that it could have been all three.

On the reverse side was a suitably cryptic message.

"Your presence is desired at the Long Marine Lab at 2 p.m. tomorrow. Please ask for Ms. DeGrazia."

There was no signature, address, or stamp.

Slocum called Greg, the most likely source of anything peculiar in his life.

"Hey, somebody put a postcard of a two-headed pig in my mailbox," Slocum reported.

"I hate it when that happens."

"Was it you?"

"No. I saw a two-headed calf once, though, at the Ripley's Museum in St. Augustine, Florida. It was stuffed."

"Did it look happy?" Slocum asked.

"Hmm. That's a hard question. Young bovine mood interpretation is kind of a specialized field."

"The pig seemed upset."

"I'm sorry."

Slocum read Greg the postcard's message.

"Sounds like a potential adventure," his friend told him.

"Exactly. Who needs it?"

"Well, you never know. It might be a beautiful woman who's been admiring you from afar."

"From where?"

"Afar. That's where anonymous people always admire from. I think it's in New Jersey."

"So you'd go, huh?"

"Absolutely. What's the worst thing that could happen?"

"I get press-ganged into an oceanographic expedition? Eaten by mutant marine life?"

"Hey, I like those, Slocum. Those are good. But I was thinking maybe it would be a prank and nothing would happen when you got there. Big deal, right? That's not so bad. That's all you're risking and it might be something great. After all, whoever it is has imagination. A two-headed pig — that's no ordinary postcard."

"That's true. But don't we have a class tomorrow afternoon?"

"Mooney's away this week — remember?" Greg reminded him.

"Oh yeah. Well, what the hell."

"Atta boy."

And thus the two-headed pig ushered in a new era in Slocum's life. What had been hard was about to become much harder.

* * *

The dolphin pool at Long Marine Lab appeared to Slocum to be almost supernaturally round. He couldn't remember ever encountering anything so perfectly circular; it struck him as being a very odd thing. Why would anyone bother to build it that way? It seemed so unlikely that Slocum wondered if it was just him — the mood he was in. Sometimes things seemed to be charged with a perfectness that he couldn't explain.

The lab was a jumble of trailers, decks, small wooden buildings, and greenhouses situated on a scrubby plateau a few hundred yards from the Pacific at the north end of the city. Slocum had assumed that he would need to show someone the postcard he'd received or otherwise explain himself to gain entry. The lab was a research branch of the University of California system, and wasn't open to the public. But the few people Slocum spied on his way in paid him no mind at all. He was a bit disappointed by this; he had psyched himself up to tell his tale, even to unleash a few carefully thought out witticisms.

A young woman was standing by the edge of the pool. The sun was behind her, robbing her of detail. Slocum spoke to her silhouette as he advanced across the pebbled cement patio.

"Excuse me," he called. "Is Ms. DeGrazia around?"

The woman pivoted suddenly and slapped a hand to her heart. Slocum moved out of the line of the sun, transforming the woman into three lovely dimensions.

"Whoa," she exhaled. "You scared the hell out of me."

"I'm sorry."

Slocum was having trouble breathing too. The woman was a stunning green-eyed blonde in her mid twenties. She wore a one-piece black bathing suit and purple sweatpants rolled up to her knees. Her features were strong, especially her mouth, which was wide and full lipped. She wasn't wearing any make-up and she didn't need any. She had freckles, lots of freckles. The ones on her cheeks wandered down her neck and into the vee of her breasts. Alongside this, the woman's hand, still cupped over her heart, was strangely white. The fingers were long and spidery, as though they rested on an invisible web.

"I guess I walk quietly," Slocum acknowledged, crossing his arms and widening his stance.

The woman raised her arms and tucked a few stray yellow hairs into her ponytail. "I guess so," she replied, smiling. "What was that you were asking?"

"I'm looking for Ms. DeGrazia. Do you know where I can find her?"

"Sure don't. Fran doesn't work here any more."

"Oh." Slocum wasn't sure what to do next.

"Can I help you?" the woman offered. She seemed genuinely concerned about him.

"Well, I don't know. It's kind of weird," Slocum admitted.

"This is Santa Cruz." The woman smiled with her eyes this time.

"Good point."

He pulled the postcard of the two-headed pig out of his green polo shirt pocket and handed it over. As the woman studied it, Slocum coerced his eyes away from her and glanced around. The water in the pool to his left was grayish blue and very calm. Beyond it he could see the rocky cliffs that formed the interface between the land and the sea. From the pool area he could clearly see inland, too. The university sat poised above the town almost directly east of the lab. Most of it was hidden in redwood groves, but the buildings sprawling in the lower meadows implied a spillage problem. It was as though the university was beginning to leak down into the town, polluting it with some obscure academic waste product.

"You're right," the woman agreed, handing back the card. "This is weird. I don't know anything about it."

Just then the surface of the pool's water was ripped asunder and three gleaming dolphins soared up into the sunlight.

"Eeeee!" the sleek fliers shrieked in unison.

They were huge. Beautiful. Awe-inspiring. Slocum had never been so close to anything so magical and powerful. The immediacy and intensity of the experience bypassed his mind; he felt as though the raw sensory input was bombarding his gut. He was too overwhelmed to tell his feet to move, but they stepped back on their own as the dolphins seemed to hover in mid-air. Then, just as suddenly as they had appeared, the fliers crash-landed in the pool, spraying the patio with gallons of cold sea water. Miraculously, the deluge completely missed Slocum. A small area encircling him remained dry while everything else, including the woman, was thoroughly drenched. The air was awash with tangy, oceanic odors, and it was suddenly very quiet.

"Wow!" the lab worker exclaimed without moving, her voice lower than before.

"Do they do that a lot?" Slocum asked.

"They never do that. I mean, they never have before." She shifted her eyes from the pool to his eyes, as though some explanation might be found there.

"How do they know how to control the splash?" Slocum asked. "I mean there were three of them. That's a lot to coordinate."

The young woman paused before answering. "I don't know. None of this is part of their normal behavior pattern. I guess that...."

The dolphins interrupted her by poking their heads up at poolside and squealing soulfully.

"What about that?" Slocum asked. "They do that, right?" The woman shook her head slowly, her eyes widening. She seemed to be progressing from a moderate personal epiphany to a true religious experience.

Turning his attention to the dolphins, Slocum stepped forward and crouched over the noisy animals. With just their heads out of the water, the dolphins presented a much more manageable sensory experience. Slocum even noticed differences between the three. One's head was rounder than the others, one's eyes were a bit bigger, and the third one was substantially smaller than the other two. The noises they were making sounded the way a two-headed pig might sound if it were skinnier, smarter, and sported a third head.

"Hi guys," Slocum said, reaching out a hand to pat them as he would a dog. As he touched the closest snout, the dolphin's noise — language? — rose in pitch and took on an unearthly tone. Somehow in the broad-banded sound there was simultaneously a cry, a laugh, and a shout. As he stroked the others, they emitted the same affecting shriek. Slocum was disconcerted, but their skin — was it skin? — felt so amazingly smooth that he continued stroking them until the woman pulled his arm away.

"That's enough," she told him. "They can't take any more."

Slocum stood; the dolphins slid back into the depths of the pool.

"Can't take any more what? I was just patting them."

The woman blushed. It started on her neck and spread upwards. She rubbed one of her ears and looked away as she replied. "I don't know why, but they were coming. That's the noise they make when they come."

"You're kidding."

Her dark green eyes returned to his. Solemnly, she shook her head. "No, I'm definitely not kidding. Who *are* you?"

Slocum held out his hand. "Slocum Happler," he told her.

The woman studied his hand and then grinned. "I'm not sure I'm ready for this."

Slocum smiled back. "It doesn't work on women. Hell, nothing does. What's your name?"

The woman grabbed his hand. "Lucy Griffin. Can I have your phone number?" She blushed again. "I mean I have a friend who's doing research on the three stooges here." She gestured with a long, elegant thumb at the now-placid water in the pool. "He asked me to keep a lookout for anyone they react to in an unusual way."

"Do you think I qualify?"

Lucy just stared at him and Slocum wasn't sure why but he found himself laughing. The lab worker smiled tolerantly but remained so clearly on-task about the phone number that Slocum momentarily doubted her stated motive. He was by no means ugly or crippled, and after all he was now capable of elevating sea animals to ecstasy with a casual touch. Maybe Lucy was just bowled over by him. This thought exterminated his laughter; Slocum told her his phone number. "Can you remember numbers?" he asked. "I can't."

"It's no problem," she assured him. "I'm a scientist."

There was a pause, during which Slocum surveyed the uncanny roundness of the pool again. If it was just his mood, it certainly had proven to be a durable one.

"What are you doing later?" Lucy asked, folding her arms across her wet bathing suit.

"Uh, I don't know. Why?"

"We could meet for dinner and maybe my friend could drop by. He's a really interesting guy."

Slocum couldn't imagine why such a beautiful woman would think that she needed any additional inducement to attract a dinner partner. Lucy misunderstood his delay in responding.

"I guess I'm being pushy," she said, but her tone didn't match her words.

"No, no," Slocum told her. "I was thinking how lucky I am. I'd love to meet you for dinner. Do you like Mexican food?"

Lucy nodded.

"El Zapoteca?" they both suggested simultaneously.

Two

Slocum's concept of adventure entailed using an unfamiliar brand of ketchup on his french fries or perhaps peeing into an odd-shaped urinal if it was absolutely necessary. Santa Cruz's idea of adventure managed to supersede this viewpoint on a daily basis. A stroll downtown might furnish several intense encounters with militant street people who felt they were entitled to Slocum's spare change. Even less palatable were the packs of confrontive youths who sported bizarre haircuts, colorful tattoos, and tended to pierce unlikely body parts such as tongues. To Slocum, their behavior was as unpredictable as the local weather.

You could travel as little as a mile and find yourself in a totally different microclimate with a fifteen degree temperature differential. A favorite trick of Santa Cruz, California was to present the sun, con you into a pair of shorts and a tee shirt, and then invite in a cool fog from the adjacent Monterey Bay. This kind of thing did help to pinpoint the tourists in the resort town. They were the ones that weren't dressed in easily removable layers, often exhibiting prodigious goosebumps.

And then there were the earthquakes; you couldn't even count on the damn ground to stay still.

Slocum knew he wasn't just paranoid. Other people said the same thing. There was something about Santa Cruz that challenged you, that elicited your unresolved issues and pushed them in your face. You couldn't stay stuck; you were moved along. The choice was whether to yield gracefully to the process or be dragged forward kicking and screaming. After fourteen months in town, Slocum hadn't settled on a personal strategy yet. Yielding seemed kind of wimpy, but it was becoming clear that resistance was useless. His ambivalence translated into a sort of graceless yielding, fraught with busy-mindedness and self-pity. It didn't help that Slocum lived alone and wasn't in a relationship. Sometimes he yearned for someone to witness the difficulties in his life and listen patiently to whatever whining he might indulge in. Someone with a big heart. And breasts — any size would do. His friend Greg suggested he place a personal ad.

"Wanted: SWF to witness suffering and be a target for self-indulgent behavior. Special attention paid to chest area, internally and externally. Don't miss this opportunity."

Slocum did not pursue his friend's suggestion, although he remained ready to prey on such a person should she wander into his life. At twenty-nine, after three major relationships, Slocum felt primed for one that actually worked.

Sometimes he wondered if he had room in his life for anyone. Partly, this was a sensible concern based on his miniscule living space. Slocum rented a 1920's beach cottage that had apparently been constructed to the specifications of a smaller race of people. Perhaps there had been an early twentieth-century pygmy immigration that had escaped the history books. Only the living room was large enough to be called small. The kitchen was an alcove, the bathroom a jigsaw puzzle of fixtures, and the bedroom just barely accommodated Slocum's bed. The one closet in the place balked at caretaking more than five or six hangered garments. Fortunately, there was an oversized plywood doghouse in the backyard that Slocum could use as a storage shed.

The outside of the rectangular cottage was mostly dilapidated dark green clapboard, but the paint had blistered, revealing a yellow undercoating, which, in turn, yielded patches of faded pink paint. The combination looked like an array of psychedelic abscesses.

Actually, Slocum enjoyed living there. The price was right, it was only four blocks from Seabright Beach, and at five foot nine it wasn't as though he was some kind of giant anyway.

Slocum was a graduate student in the History of Consciousness program at U.C. Santa Cruz, commonly known as HistCon. His friend, Greg, at twenty-one, was the youngest student in the department. He was also from Santa Cruz, which was a rarity up on campus. Greg had whizzed through the University of Texas as an undergraduate, then returned home for grad school. Slocum grew up in Austin, Texas, which he thought of as a lovely place to escape from. But Texas had been the initial commonality that had launched the friendship between the seemingly dissimilar pair.

Greg was gangly, six-foot four, and blue eyed, with an unruly blond beard and a peculiar haircut. A semicircle on the back of his head was very long and he braided it down his back. The rest was extremely short — maybe an inch and a half long — and it bunched and stuck up in spikes. Make him surly, give him more outrageous clothes, and Greg would fit right in with the downtown denizens.

Slocum wore his black curly hair just over his ears and usually shaved twice a day. Caterpillar-like eyebrows lurked over his light gray eyes, and the rest of his face suggested an air of competence, although this impression wasn't especially accurate. He was handsome in an old-fashioned way that he considered too bland. Slocum's nose and mouth didn't proclaim his character, for example; they were merely regularly shaped, functional, and situated at the lower end of his face. He was especially bored by his nose, which might have suited a fourteen-year-old girl, but was too small and ordinary to please Slocum.

Professors tended to dislike both Greg and Slocum; women appreciated one or the other of them. Children were usually more drawn to the darker, smaller man, while pets split on the issue. Cats preferred Greg, and dogs favored Slocum.

On another level, none of this mattered. Behind their eyes, the two men lived in complementary inner worlds. It wasn't something they talked about, but both Slocum and Greg sensed some sort of deep, complex connection. One manifestation of this phenomenon was a comfortability with one another, an ease of being that allowed room for practically anything. Slocum appreciated this more than Greg, who was less limited by the usual pantheon of social inhibitions in the first place. Greg could express his feelings to a stranger in a bank line and then invite the teller out for dinner. A girlfriend had dumped him once because she said he had lousy boundaries, but Slocum was envious of his friend's ability.

Greg, in turn, admired Slocum a great deal in several respects. Sometimes the self-exiled Texan displayed a knack for knowing what was going on in other people's heads. From Slocum's perspective it felt like sensing a pattern that the hidden information completed. It just seemed sometimes that other people's stuff would only fit into the moment if it were a particular way. He wasn't always right, and he didn't value it as much as Greg did. But there wasn't a much better way to impress a date than to trot out his knack and let her misinterpret it as being indicative of his deeply sensitive nature.

Another unusual feature of Slocum's personality was his ability to maintain his objectivity when facing a highly charged issue. There was a place in his mind he could usually retreat to where he wasn't pushed around by his personal history or his feelings. Of course he abused the power of this sanctuary by plugging objectivity into a variety of situations which actually required feelings and such. Slocum's physical coordination was another quality that Greg admired. The slightly built Slocum wasn't tall or abnormally strong, but sports came easily to him, and he rarely lost in any sort of physical competition.

Three

Later, in his elderly Volvo en route to the restaurant, Slocum could barely remember the details of his afternoon encounter. It had all been so anomalous that his mind seemed to have filed it away as a dream or a fantasy. This was the usual sort of Santa Cruz perversity. When something great happened, it was relatively inaccessible for enjoyable replay. When disaster struck, he couldn't pry it out of the forefront of his consciousness no matter what he did.

El Zapoteca was a small, noisy place on south Pacific Avenue, an area that hadn't fared too badly in the 1989 earthquake. Across the street was an intact New Age bookstore, and next door was a futon shop in which squads of neo-hippies made the futons by hand behind tasteful Japanese screens. Only two doors up Santa Cruz's main street, on the other hand, an anachronistic auto parts store displayed a poster of a sleepy-eyed girl in a sequined gold bikini sitting astride an eight-ball gear shift.

The restaurant itself was allied with the traditional element in town. Only a yellowed, hand-lettered sign in a corner of the window stating "We welcome students" hinted that Santa Cruz wasn't the same sleepy fishing village it had been when El Zapoteca had first opened in the nineteen-fifties. The interior was unabashedly corny-Mexican with big, festive hats on the walls and colored Christmas lights strung everywhere. A series of black velvet paintings featured large-breasted Aztec maidens being carried off by an assortment of super-macho warriors. The waitresses, bulky middle-aged women, wore colorful native garb, and to complete the cunning illusion of an exotic south-of-the-border experience, a garish jukebox constantly blared out Mexican music.

Lucy was waiting in a red vinyl booth by the front window. She wore a man's white dress shirt and well-worn jeans. Her blond hair was braided and coiled on her head. On someone else it would've looked contrived; on Lucy it was elegant, almost royal. Slocum began smiling as soon as he saw her.

He was wearing brown corduroy jeans and a cobalt blue cotton sweater. These were the clothes he felt most comfortable in, and they placed him high on the fashion hierarchy at El Zapoteca that evening.

"Sorry I'm late," Slocum said as he slid onto the lumpy bench seat across from Lucy.

"You're not."

"Sorry you're early."

"That's better. I'm sorry too," Lucy confessed. "I'm always early for everything."

"Why not just leave a little later?"

"Psychology is just a little more complicated than that, Slocum."

"I'll consider myself rebuked," Slocum commented, instantly regretting what he'd said. It was so pretentious.

The waitress appeared and distributed giant laminated menus, Slocum hid behind his and regrouped. There was about as much actual salsa on the menu as there were printed items. He picked off a small chunk of hot pepper and decided on the combination platter that was under it. Then he covertly observed his dinner companion from around the edge of the menu.

Lucy's expression was very studious. Perhaps her meal selections fell into the same category for her as library research or selecting a birth control method. Slocum's sister was like that. She practically became paralyzed over the small, arbitrary decisions that constituted the nuts and bolts of living. Slocum had always assumed that her behavior was related to some delusion she had about controlling what happened to her. If she just picked the right brand of cereal at the grocery store, maybe she would never have to worry about tornadoes — that sort of thing.

As Slocum watched, a tear squeezed out of one of Lucy's eyes and he amended his evaluation. Maybe menus were akin to

Russian novels for her. Or perhaps her family had owned a beautiful restaurant that had been bombed by anarchists.

Lucy glanced up and noticed his attention. She casually wiped away the solitary tear. "I have overactive tear ducts," she told him. "My eyes think there's foreign matter in them that needs washing out. But there isn't."

"I've never heard of that."

"It's rare, but it runs in my family. Well, actually tear duct *problems* run in the family. Everybody else has the opposite problem."

"You mean they can't cry?"

"No. I mean their eyes dry out unless they apply artificial tears every so often."

"I've never heard of that, either," Slocum told her.

"It's a lot more common. They sell artificial tears right in drugstores. What are you having?"

"Uh, the number three combo."

"Don't you hate that word 'combo'?"

"No," Slocum confessed. "I like it; I like saying it. Combo! It's fun."

There was a pause. Slocum began wondering if his liking the word 'combo' was going to present a serious problem for Lucy.

"What are you having?" he finally asked.

"Number six."

"What's that?"

"I don't remember." Lucy arched forward, her green eyes gleaming. "Why did the dolphins go nuts over you?"

Slocum leaned back against the old tuck and roll upholstery. He'd been nibbling at that question for hours but hadn't mustered any answers or even generated one viable theory. He decided to shrug, but halfway through the motion his mouth sabotaged his plan and said, "Maybe it's shakti." This idea was news to him; he was barely familiar with the term.

"Energy? Spiritual energy?"

Slocum decided to nod and this time his body parts cooperated nicely.

"You might be right," Lucy responded. "I've noticed that the three stooges seem to like or dislike people independent of the kind of criteria that people use. Maybe they tune into energy."

The waitress reappeared. Despite her size, the gray-haired woman had a real knack for suddenly manifesting next to the table.

"Can I help you?" she intoned woodenly.

They ordered, surrendered their menus, and were left alone again.

"So you think dolphins are psychic?" Slocum asked.

Lucy tapped her spoon until it settled sideways onto her knife, forming a cross. "In a sense, I think everything's psychic."

Slocum considered that remark carefully. "Wouldn't you say that's going a little too far?" he asked, feeling sure that he had phrased his question as diplomatically as possible.

Lucy shook her head and smiled enigmatically.

"How about the napkin? It's psychic?"

"Not really. Let me explain."

"My Uncle Joel? Armadillos?"

"Calm down, Slocum." Lucy propped herself on her elbows and looked directly into his eyes as she spoke. "I believe that everything has consciousness — even so-called inanimate objects. Their form of it is just more rudimentary. I also believe that all consciousness is connected to all other consciousness. So being psychic is just using the connection — being conscious about the way things already are. Theoretically, everything could wise up and sense all this any time. Realistically, only higher-order consciousness has the capacity to pierce the veil. But you're not really any different than an armadillo — it's just that you ended up with a more complex arrangement of the same stuff."

"I'm a snappier dresser too," Slocum pointed out.

Lucy just gazed at him evenly, waiting.

"I thought you said you were a scientist," Slocum reminded her.

Lucy shrugged, her breasts rising and falling in a way that completely distracted him.

"So what do you think?" she asked.

He certainly didn't feel comfortable expressing his rumination that she didn't appear to be wearing a bra. He managed to say, "Very interesting," though. This failed to satisfy Lucy.

"No, really. I want to know. Does that sound totally crazy to you?"

Slocum gathered himself and sat up straight. "No, not totally." He smiled at her. "I'm actually a grad student in the HistCon program up at UCSC. So I think about this kind of thing. You design your own course of study, which in my case is mostly Western philosophy, but I've had exposure to this issue before." Lucy was smiling back at him now, apparently pleased at their coincidental interests. "There are a lot of Eastern religions that say what you said. Or at least something close. It's not like everyone living in Asia is crazy, right? It's just that for the most part these ideas don't match my experience."

"Things don't seem connected?"

"Exactly. And livestock on down seems pretty much unconscious to me, let alone my Uncle Joel."

"I'll bet you don't even have an Uncle Joel," Lucy chided, shifting to tuck her legs up under her.

"Oh believe me. He's all too real. Ask Aunt Helen. But the point I'm making is that I can't believe something that doesn't match the majority of my experience."

"Of course not. I feel the same way. But tell me about your minority experiences."

"What do you mean?"

"The ones that do match. That interests me."

A busboy placed two glasses of water in front of them. Slocum thought about Lucy's question as he drank a sip of water and then tried to twirl the mustache he'd shaved off eight months previously. Finally, he described his ability to sometimes know what someone else was thinking.

"That's it! That's what I'm talking about," Lucy replied enthusiastically.

"Well, wait a minute. I want to ask you something."

"Sure."

"You said that you only believe things that match your experience too, right?"

Lucy nodded and smiled.

"Then by implication, you've actually experienced this connectedness?"

Lucy nodded more excitedly. "It's wonderful."

"Tell me more about it."

"Sure!" She leaned back and Slocum unconsciously moved forward, maintaining the same distance between them. To Slocum it was as if no one else was in the noisy room.

"It's an overwhelming sense of everything being perfect," Lucy began, her eyes seeing past him.

"Hey, I get that sometimes."

She continued as if she hadn't heard him. "And there's this sense that it's all working together, that nothing's wrong with anything, no matter how it usually seems. It's like feeling love, only it's more of a sensory experience and less of an emotion. It's really hard to describe."

"You're doing great. It really does sound wonderful. Is it something like being on acid?"

"I don't know." Her eyes were still far away.

"Like having a vision?"

Lucy shrugged again, her chest tempting Slocum to ask an endless series of unanswerable questions.

The food arrived, though, and they both fell to it intently. It wasn't until Lucy had cleared her plate that she spoke again, and then it was just to excuse herself as she arose to head for the ladies room.

Four

Slocum sat by himself, stared at the gooey remains of his meal, and suddenly felt overwhelmed. His version of this state was comprised of confusion, elation, and insecurity. Never a maestro at accommodating paradox, Slocum was besieged by internal conflict. He decided to make a list of everything unusual that had happened so far. When something could be reduced to a few words on a list, it seemed so much more improbable that it would kick you in the balls.

Slocum's list contained six items: 'pig postcard, roundness of pool, contact with beautiful woman, unusual dolphin behavior, simultaneity of restaurant choice, and coincidence of metaphysical interests.' Upon reflection he added 'beautiful woman seems to like me.' This was a major item; it went a long way towards explaining why the others didn't disturb him even more.

List in hand, Slocum felt himself relaxing. By the time Lucy returned, maybe he'd be fairly normal, whatever that was.

Just then, a man sat down opposite him and said, "Hello, Slocum" in a rich baritone voice.

Slocum decided to write this down as item number eight on his list before looking up or replying. It didn't help.

The man across the table was extremely striking. He was probably in his mid-forties but wore his brown hair long and loose. His huge beard was an amalgamation of every natural hair color — black, brown, gray, white, and a startling shade of red. On someone else, the hairy potpourri would have dominated whatever hapless face resided above it. On this man, it was merely a temporary distraction from a pair of totally present clear brown eyes. The eyes were scary. They proclaimed that your bullshit wouldn't work, that he could see past it and actually know who you are.

Slocum stopped breathing. It was involuntary, a futile attempt to distance himself from the man.

The penetrating brown eyes were locked on his as the man spoke again.

"It's a pleasure to meet the man who pleasures dolphins," he stated and held out a large hand. "Lucas Dayton. I'm Lucy's friend."

Slocum's breath returned; he shook the hand. "Slocum Happler," he croaked. Lucas' hand was very solid. It felt as though the flesh was more fully packed than usual.

"Have you murdered Lucy?" the man asked in a perfectly reasonable tone of voice.

"Uh, no."

"Good, good. Just invisible, is she? Another little surprise in your bag of tricks?"

Slocum discovered himself to be temporarily out of words.

"I wouldn't put it past you, son." Lucas smiled an odd smile. It was more of a display of his uneven white teeth — a strategic withdrawal of his lips — than an expression of a specific emotion. Slocum had the impression that Lucas' mouth would arrange itself the same way for a grimace, for example.

Lucy returned and slid onto the bench next to her friend.

"Hi Lucas."

"Hello Lucy. Have you been enjoying your dinner?"

"So far," she replied lightly.

Lucas laughed; it was a deep, liquid sound unlike anything Slocum had ever heard. Also, the older man's delight at Lucy's comment seemed wildly out of proportion to any inherent humor. Perhaps it was an inside joke or reminded him of something else, Slocum reasoned.

"How did you recognize me?" Slocum asked Lucas.

"Well, all Lucy said was that you were cute."

Slocum glanced at her; she blushed and dropped her eyes.

" *That's* cute," Slocum told Lucas.

"I agree. At any rate, who you were was rather obvious for other reasons."

"Obvious?"

"Yes."

Lucy spoke up.

"That's not exactly an explanation, is it?"

"No," Lucas agreed amicably, displaying his multi-purpose smile facsimile. After a brief pause, the older man spoke again. "It would be better not to go into that now."

The combination of the eyes, the tone of voice, and all the other factors that go into creating presence lent this pronouncement a tremendous air of authority. Slocum didn't doubt the statement for a second, although he remained curious.

There was another pause; Slocum spoke next.

"So you're doing dolphin research?" he asked.

"Not exactly," Lucas answered. "I am an anesthesiologist by profession, but I have an interest in dolphins and an even greater interest in those whom dolphins favor. That's enough about me. May I ask you a question, Slocum?"

"Sure."

"Do you often dream about a three-story white Victorian farmhouse?"

Slocum blinked furiously; he was truly stunned. "Yes. How on earth did you know that?" he asked urgently. His list had been one version of unusual — this was something else.

Lucas waved away Slocum's concern. His gesture was spare and graceful, although this was lost on poor Slocum.

Lucy reached over and patted his hand. "Hang in there," she exhorted.

"Wait a minute," Slocum protested, pulling his hand away and crossing his arms. "This is very weird. I mean *very* weird, you know?"

Lucas gazed at him calmly. Those clear eyes seemed to already know anything Slocum might say. His mind raced. He'd never told anyone about his recurring dream except for Greg and an old girlfriend back in Texas. An explanation occurred to him and he seized it quickly.

"Greg put you two up to this, didn't he?"

"Who?" Lucy asked.

Lucas just kept watching Slocum. His expression seemed to convey that all of Slocum's potential reactions were one and the same to him.

"Come on," Slocum implored. "Give it up. This isn't funny any more."

By the time he'd finished speaking, he knew that Greg had nothing to do with whatever was going on. The words didn't ring true at all. There were too many coincidences and truly weird aspects of all this. It was beyond even Greg. You couldn't hire an actor that could play Lucas the way Lucas was playing himself, for example. No one could just invent that magnitude of presence. It was like sitting across from a completely impartial witness or a mirror. Slocum felt naked, exposed to his core.

Finally Lucas spoke. "I'm sorry, but once again it would work out better if I don't explain myself right now. Let's just say that your response affirms something quite important."

Slocum couldn't drop it. "Does everyone dream about this farmhouse at a certain stage in their development? Is that it? Can you tell I'm at that particular point or something?"

Lucas pursed and unpursed his lips rhythmically; he looked like a fish with a beard. "No," he eventually replied. "Very few people dream that dream. It's not for everyone."

"Then I don't get it," Slocum told him, frustration in his voice.

"That's true. You don't." Lucas leaned back and watched him again.

Slocum turned to Lucy. "Do you dream about farmhouses?" he asked.

She shook her head. "Dormitories mostly. But I'm working on it."

The waitress slapped down the check in front of Slocum and he jumped about a foot.

Lucas laughed his peculiar laugh, Lucy smiled, and Slocum nodded seriously. The waitress departed; he didn't notice. "Maybe this is enough for one night," Lucas suggested.

"Huh?"

"I think I'll be going," the older man told him.

"Wait."

Lucas didn't wait. Lucy moved out of his way and he strode out of the room without another word. It was quite a sight. He was tall and his hair flowed behind him as though it were a waterfall of some dense, brown liquid. Almost everyone remaining in the restaurant stopped whatever they were doing and watched him. He wore a light blue chambray work shirt, jeans, and brown work shoes, but on him it wasn't a casual ensemble. It was like a uniform.

"Was Lucas in the Service?" Slocum asked.

"Yes," Lucy replied, settling in directly across from him.

"The Navy?" Slocum asked.

"Yes! How did you know?"

Slocum shrugged. His pattern-sensing didn't impress him. "I guess he always wears the same clothes, right?"

"That's right! Oh Slocum, I can see something really special happened tonight. I'm so pleased. You two have some kind of incredible connection. And Lucas really liked you, you know. I've never seen him so .... " Lucy struggled to finish her thought.

"Frustrating?" Slocum suggested. Lucy smiled.

"Scary?" he tried next.

"Open," she replied firmly.

"Open? He didn't tell me anything!"

"He let you see who he was. That's a lot more intimate than a bunch of explanations. You should be honored."

Slocum thought that over. "But I *don't* know who he is," he protested.

"Whose fault is that?" Lucy asked. "Listen, I've got to go. Shall we split the check?"

"Let's take turns," Slocum suggested. "You get the next one."

"That's a great idea." She stood and thanked him for the meal. "I'll see you again, Slocum."

"You bet. Can I get your phone number then?"

"Actually, I just moved and I haven't gotten around to getting one yet. I'll call you soon. Good night."

Slocum sat in the booth another half hour before heading home.

He almost ran over a possum on the San Lorenzo bridge. The sight of the giant rat-like creature flooded him with disgust.

Five

Slocum conceptualized various modes of dividing humanity into dichotomies. There were relatively trivial divisions, such as visor people versus non-visor people, or Pepsi drinkers versus Coke drinkers. There were more significant categories too, such as who could keep a secret, who was capable of violence, or who might sleep with Slocum some day if he played his cards right. But the foremost dichotomy Slocum had ever encountered was Lucas versus everyone else Slocum had every met. It wasn't as though the man embodied more of any particular character traits, or even better versions of them. It was as if he were singular at a more fundamental level. His attributes were his. He didn't share them with all the confused creatures milling around in the world who kind of looked like him.

These were Slocum's thoughts as he tried to fall asleep. The next morning he awoke wondering if he was overreacting to the previous day's experiences. He considered the matter for the three seconds it took to scuttle naked to the bathroom. Nope. He wasn't. During his first blissful pee of the day, the only one he ever really enjoyed, he realized that, if anything, he was underreacting. Then the phone chirped.

Terminating his pee early, leaking a bit onto the old orange carpet, Slocum stumbled into the small living room and grabbed the receiver.

"Hello?" His voice was husky with sleep.

"Good morning, Slocum," a man's voice replied smoothly.

"Is it?"

"Absolutely." The voice was sure of it.

Slocum scratched the underside of his testicles as he tried to figure out who the hell was on the phone.

"You don't know who this is, do you?" the voice said.

"Of course I do." As he ruminated further, Slocum's hand wandered into his navel and extracted a minute piece of blue lint.

"This is Lucas Dayton. I know I didn't wake you, but perhaps you need a few minutes to gather yourself. I'll call back." The phone line went dead.

Slocum replaced the receiver and meandered into the kitchen alcove. He was curiously unaffected by the call. As he procured a yogurt and a spoon, he decided not to think about it. So of course he did. It was like the game his mother had introduced to Slocum and his toddler sister one rainy afternoon — run around the table and don't think about a fox. He'd tried so hard, but he never could manage to think about anything else.

Maybe he was blase about Lucas' call because he was numbed by the onslaught of odd events. Maybe he was still half asleep. Maybe he....

The yogurt was spoiled; he rushed to the sink and spat out a mouthful. Suddenly he felt overwhelmingly nauseated. He fought back the rising bile as he leaned over the drain. It was more than just the bad yogurt. Something inside really wanted to get out. It was a feeling he'd never experienced before — almost a need to vomit psychologically as well as physically.

Somehow he made it back to bed, where he lay face down and tried to sink back into sleep.

The phone chirped again. Why, wondered Slocum, did cheap phones sound like angry crickets? He let it continue for at least half a minute, then he struggled to his bare feet and answered it in the living room. "Hello?"

"How are you feeling, Slocum?" It was Lucas again.

"I feel like I need to barf up everything inside me, including my brain."

Lucas laughed. "That's terrific."

"Thanks a lot." He slumped onto his decrepit green loveseat and closed his eyes.

"Think how much room you'd be making," Lucas added.

"Room?" Slocum draped his arm across his forehead, the inside of his elbow resting on his third eye.

"If you're full already, where's the new stuff going to fit?"

Slocum began to get irritated; there was an edge to his voice when he replied, "Make up your mind. Do you want to laugh at my pain or share vague philosophical asides?"

"Both!" Lucas proclaimed, exercising his peculiar laugh.

Slocum sat up, held the receiver away from his ear, and waited for the laughter to subside.

"Look," he began. "It's early, I feel sick, and I have some things to do. I'm not trying to be rude, but exactly why did you call?"

"I know someone who can help you get a handle on the energy experiences you had yesterday."

"You mean with the dolphins?"

"Exactly. He's an Indian man — a yogi. This kind of thing is right up his alley."

Lucas' liberal use of idioms seemed peculiar to Slocum. Somehow he'd thought that the man was beyond such inelegant language.

"What does yoga have to do with energy?" he asked.

"Everything. Essentially, it's the study of energy and how to manipulate it."

"I thought it was stretching and doing postures," Slocum told him.

"Those are means to an end, my friend. Now normally you have to make an appointment months in advance, but I pulled a few strings and he'll see you at ten this morning."

Once again the idiomatic phrasing jangled; it was as if Lucas was deliberately choosing words that made him sound more ordinary.

"What's his name?" Slocum asked.

"Baba Ahimsa. It means 'Father of love.' His followers call him 'Baba'."

"Is that the Cruz Mountain guy?"

"Exactly."

There was a spiritual community that lived on top of a ridge about twenty-five miles south of Santa Cruz. They had their own school, fire department, and organic farm. The article in the Santa Cruz Sentinel that Slocum had read had been entitled 'Cruz Mountain Yoga Center is the Real McCoy.' He had pictured an inbred-looking guru in overalls and a straw hat aiming a musket at a Hatfield hillbilly. Unfortunately, this image was about all he remembered.

"Slocum?" Lucas prompted.

"Uh huh."

"It will work out best if I drive you up."

"Okay."

"Can you meet me at the Town Clock at nine?"

"Sure."

"Great. And let me ask you something. How do you feel now?"

Slocum took stock, moving his awareness down from his head back into his body.

"Fine?" he tried, disbelieving it himself. It was true, though. Everything was back to normal.

"I thought so. See you soon."

Slocum said goodbye to the dead line and wandered back into the kitchen, ready for a second try at breakfast.

*   *   *

At a quarter to nine, Slocum hopped on his old Motobecane racing bike and wheeled onto East Cliff Drive for the two mile ride downtown. The morning fog was thicker than usual. Until it burned off around noon, the temperature would remain cool in Santa Cruz. Slocum liked the fog. It softened the edges of everything and lent a magical ambiance to life.

The Town Clock stood at the opposite end of Pacific Avenue from El Zapoteca, marking the northern border of the business district. Serving a population of about fifty thousand, Santa Cruz's downtown encompassed a three-block by eight-block rectangle, although a good third of it was still rubble. The snail's pace of rebuilding after the big quake was one of the hot topics at the many wildly pretentious coffee houses in town.

Originally, the wood and brick clock tower had roosted atop a historic building, now it squatted on its own in a small plaza. It was a gathering place for the town's homeless, formerly known as 'trolls' since they camped under bridges in inclement weather. Politically correct Santa Cruz had switched to 'homeless' virtually the instant it became hip. Greg speculated that the next word swap might be 'housing impaired.' He also readily furnished an extensive tirade about the absurdity of the term 'politically correct' whenever granted the opportunity.

As Slocum neared the tower, he saw that a ragged assemblage of perhaps twenty people was protesting that morning. This wasn't unusual, but instead of condemning police harassment, this time the crude banners declared that Santa Cruz's homeless population was against thought control.

"Me too," Slocum told the hulking, fetid schizophrenic who stared at his silver bike as he dismounted. He decided to lock it up somewhere out of sight. When he returned, Lucas was standing at parade rest exactly where Slocum had been a moment before. He was wearing his customary blue chambray work shirt, jeans, and brown work boots. The schizophrenic was on his knees, hugging one of Lucas' legs.

Slocum strolled up and spoke first. "You know, when I moved to Santa Cruz, I couldn't pick a crazy person out of a crowd of... well, whatever group passes for sane. Now I can diagnose at a glance."

"And what do you say about our friend here?" Lucas asked. As he spoke, the long-haired, bearded homeless man looked up, nodding and squinting furiously. Other homeless people, men and women, marched desultorily near the trio, brandishing cardboard signs.

"Schizophrenic," Slocum pronounced.

Lucas reached down and placed his hand on the man's greasy head as though he were palming a basketball. Closing his eyes, he froze for just a moment, then revived and spoke.

"You're right."

"Is it written in braille on his head?" Slocum asked.

Lucas chortled. The man clutching him became alarmed and scrabbled away to the other side of the clock tower.

"You're just about the only person that addresses me in that manner," Lucas told Slocum. "It's very refreshing."

"So what were you doing?"

Lucas moved forward and placed his heavy arm across Slocum's shoulder, guiding him towards the curb. "I'm a doctor, remember?" he chided lightly. The expression on his face invited his listener to accept this non-answer. Slocum acquiesced.

Lucas drove a full-sized black Chevy pick-up truck, which once again confounded Slocum's expectations. This was what Texans in shitkicker boots tooled around in looking for cheap beer.

"I don't even drink or hunt," Lucas told him as they climbed up onto the black vinyl bench seat.

"Before we go," Slocum replied, "I want to know something. Do you read minds?"

"Hardly ever. I intuit patterns. I know how things have to be. Do you understand?"

"Actually, I think I do."

As Lucas started the truck, he tapped a cassette into the stereo, effectively terminating conversation. It was Mozart — a concerto with an oboe or a clarinet. Just recently, Slocum had realized that he enjoyed classical music.

He sat back and let the sound surround him. After a few miles, he felt himself relax. As the south county scenery reminded him of what a beautiful part of the world he lived in, Slocum gradually became content to let his latest adventure unfold as it would.

Six

Up on the ridge, forty minutes later, Lucas maneuvered the truck onto the dirt shoulder of the narrow road and switched off the music. While the Chevy idled its growly V-8 powerplant, he swiveled his head and focused his penetrating gaze onto Slocum.

"The gate is just ahead on the left," he told him. "It would be best if you walked in on your own."

"Why is that?"

"There is power in symbolism and metaphor. Genuine power. Do you understand?"

"No."

"It doesn't matter." He lightly waved away the concern.

"It does to me," Slocum asserted, his head darting forward on his neck, pigeon style.

"You'll be late," Lucas replied calmly. "It's time to part company.

"So you're not coming in at all?"

Lucas shook his head, his multi-colored beard swaying gently across his upper chest.

"So I'm just going to stroll on in and hope I bump into some older guy that looks smart? Is that it?"

Lucas smiled. Slocum waited, but that was the extent of the older man's response. With a sigh, he groped for the door handle.

"Can you be back here at eleven?" Lucas asked.

"Okay," Slocum agreed as he climbed down out of the cab. "And listen, thanks for your help. I don't mean to be ungrateful. It's just that some of this is really frustrating."

"I understand, Slocum. Just remember that your old sense of being in charge of your own life is an illusion anyway."

Lucas paused and then held up his right hand and positioned it just in front of his right shoulder. As he continued to speak, his fingers writhed like individual snakes. It wasn't sign language, but Slocum sensed that the bizarre movements were purposeful. It was the same way you could somehow differentiate an unfamiliar language from mere nonsensical babbling.

"We are just making explicit," Lucas continued, "something that pre-existed our meeting."

The fingers went wild during 'pre-existed.' Apparently the movements bore a relationship to the words or concepts Lucas elucidated. Slocum found it nearly impossible to listen while all this was transpiring. Half in and half out of the truck, he struggled to capture the meaning of his ongoing experience.

"Everything is simply the way it is, regardless of how we perceive it or organize it," was the next pronouncement. The accompanying finger dance was relatively sedate. "Few beings are in contact with reality — have a working relationship with 'what is.' So 'control' is almost always illusory. It manipulates that which is thought to be, but isn't."

Lucas shivered and slowly lowered his hand, which continued to perform its movement pattern until it finally rested on his blue-jeaned knee.

Slocum was incapable of speech by now. Whatever was going on was more than he was prepared to deal with. He started to close the truck's door, realized that would be impolite, and decided to at least say goodbye, but nothing emerged from his throat. The History of Consciousness program hadn't adequately addressed fingers, it wasn't *his* fault.

"You'd better get moving," Lucas told him. "We'll talk about this another time."

Slocum managed to nod and then swing the door closed. The truck began moving immediately. In a few seconds it had disappeared around a sharp curve.

Slocum plopped down on the paved edge of the country road. It might make him late, but he needed an opportunity to refocus himself.

The sun was out on Cruz Mountain. The temperature was in the mid-sixties and a slight westerly breeze blew in across a brown, grassy field. Slocum smelled the ocean for just a second, although he was probably ten miles inland. Then the air was arid and dusty again. October was the end of the dry season in Northern California. Areas haunted by coastal fog remained somewhat green, but the ridge was uniformly brown except for a few scattered redwood groves. Slocum's first summer in the area had been particularly dry; he had believed that everything brown was dead. It had been extremely depressing to view the hills, fields, and valleys as vast plant cemeteries. Actually, the color change was just a normal seasonal adjustment of the native flora. When the rains came in November, the transformation back to green was swift.

No traffic interrupted the process of Slocum reconnecting with his environment. It was quiet enough to hear insects, and not a single guru pestered him. Sometimes doing nothing at all was just what the doctor ordered, Slocum realized. Normally he avoided it at all costs. Boredom was so painful for Slocum that he had conditioned himself into a phobia of unstructured time. In this instance, it was with regret that he pushed himself erect and marched to the Cruz Mountain Yoga Center gate.

The ranch-style metal gate was open and a rutted dirt road wound slightly downhill on the far side of it. Only one small sign announced the presence of the community. It was a simple, hand-carved wooden plaque, which Slocum stooped to touch, although he didn't know why. Maybe it was something symbolic.

He set out down the road, striding with an appearance of confidence that he didn't feel. He was wearing white volleyball shoes, jeans, and a button-down yellow dress shirt. He wondered if this would instantly brand him as an outsider. Did everyone at the center wear special robes? Would he commit a horrible faux pas by saying or doing something prohibited? He had almost no idea what to expect. His emotions were equally split between fear and exhilaration. It felt as though either one could suddenly flip to the other, depending on what happened.

About a quarter mile further, after passing through two small meadows and several towering redwood groves, Slocum encountered his first Cruz Mountain resident. The man wore ordinary street clothes and seemed to be in a hurry. He was practically running up the road. He was about forty years old, and to Slocum he embodied the physical characteristics of an ancient Roman. He was swarthy, hirsute, Roman-nosed, and he exhibited an arrogant bearing.

"Excuse me," Slocum hailed. "Where could I find Baba? I have an appointment with him."

The man halted and then examined Slocum before responding. "Really? He normally only sees people on Saturday." He peered out of deep-set brown eyes and frowned at Slocum sternly. Slocum was reminded of a wolverine he'd watched being mounted at the zoo once. It was just about the same expression.

"Well," the man finally replied. "This time of day he's usually working in the north meadow. You go another few hundred yards and there's a trail on the right. Follow it until you come to an outhouse, then make a left."

The man scurried forward.

"Can I ask you one more thing?" Slocum said.

"What?" The man turned impatiently.

"What does Baba look like? How will I know him?"

This completely dumfounded the man; his jaw actually dropped. "You mean you don't even know what he looks like?"

Slocum shook his head and tried to appear contrite, unaware that he looked constipated at best. When the man continued to stand there and study his face, Slocum shrugged as well. If he could've thought of any more gestures, he would have tried them.

"Well, don't worry," the man told him. "You'll know him when you see him. Listen, I've really got to run. Good luck."

"Thanks!" Slocum called to his back.

Following the directions, Slocum passed several more people, a few classrooms, and a parking lot full of yellow Ford Escorts.

This would've seemed very weird a few days ago, thought Slocum. Now, a squadron of stubby cars at a rural yoga center was not a particularly surreal experience. Hell, they weren't even orgasming.

After turning at the outhouse, a two-seater with handbills plastered on the doors, Slocum paused to appreciate the view. He was one switchback above a field that was criss-crossed with low, limestone walls. Beyond the field was a magnificent panorama — all that lay between the ridge and a horizon that extended several miles into the ocean. The farms and orchards surrounding Watsonville organized the land into complex patterns featuring various hues of green and brown. The south county town itself was actually picturesque from such a distance, too. In proximity, Watsonville was a shabby, poorly zoned mish-mash of food processing plants, businesses, and modest homes, inhabited mainly by poor Hispanics. From Cruz Mountain, the collection of buildings looked to Slocum as if they'd been dropped from God's hand, scattering balmily and settling in just the right spots. This notion startled him; he was not accustomed to generating theistic images. Maybe the conversations with Lucy and Lucas were percolating, letting loose a bubble of new attitudes now and then.

The Pacific Ocean comprised a good portion of the view. From where Slocum stood, it was a uniform shade of light blue and appeared to be perfectly placid. All the detail — the dark floating kelp, the constantly churning surf — was lost to the eye. Slocum was reminded of how the sun had silhouetted Lucy at the dolphin pool. Nature could withhold or offer itself as it fancied, it seemed.

Returning his gaze to the foreground and more practical concerns, Slocum noticed a group of eight or ten people working at the far end of the field. He resumed walking and in a few minutes was down on the grassy meadow.

There didn't seem to be any path that circumvented the array of stone walls, so Slocum just climbed over all the ones that were on line to his destination. As he drew closer, he saw that the group of people were in the process of piling limestone up to form a new wall. There was no implied function or pattern to the ones he'd traversed so far. He saw no evidence that livestock had ever been penned in by the crude three-foot-high walls, for example. Perhaps they spelled out "yoga lovers welcome aliens" to passing UFOs.

The rocks in the walls were loosely piled; there was no mortar. After Slocum momentarily lost his footing on the third to last wall, he decided just to jump the final two. The work crew turned to watch his athletic entrance.

In the middle of the group stood a very short, very slight man with dark skin and bright white buck teeth. He wore a white dress and inexpensive brown beach sandals. Through the lightweight cotton, Slocum could make out red boxer shorts, which pretty much ruined the dramatic effect for him. Baba could've been anywhere from sixty to ninety. His wispy beard and long, thin hair were gray with streaks of white. His skin was stretched taut over prominent facial bones; there was just enough flesh to cover everything inside. And although he was somewhat wrinkled, the Indian man didn't display the usual configuration of age cues--crow's feet at the eyes, for instance. The eyes themselves were no help in estimating his age. They were a rich, liquid black. Paradoxically, they sparkled in the sunlight. In a way, they looked more like an animal's eyes than a man's. There was no guile or complexity in them, just innocence, or wonder, or maybe even love.

Slocum could feel his poise ebbing with each breath. He tore his eyes away from Baba and examined his followers. Most of the four men and three women were smiling at him, perhaps in remembrance of other initial meetings with their leader. They seemed to be in their forties and fifties, which surprised Slocum, who had expected a younger population. They wore various types of work clothes and gray canvas gloves. Piles of limestone rocks lay by their feet.

"I'm sorry to interrupt," Slocum began, addressing no one in particular. "But I have an appointment with Baba at ten. My name is Slocum Happler."

The yogi smiled sweetly and gently tapped himself on the sternum with a wiry index finger.

"I figured you were you," Slocum told him. "Is there some place we can talk?"

Baba lithely stepped over the half-built wall and set out at a furious pace. Slocum hurried to follow.

Seven

So far, Slocum was struck by the dissimilarity between Baba Ahimsa and Lucas Dayton. The yogi's presence was light and easy, and although his silence was slightly unsettling, Slocum wasn't nearly as intimidated or awed as he had been by Lucas. In fact, perversely, it was Baba's lack of forcefulness that inspired what fear Slocum did feel. There were no mysterious sub-components in the Indian man, no sense that he was anything besides exactly how he presented in the moment. This gave an impression of extreme one-pointedness. Were he to look at you, all of him would be looking. That "all of him" seemed to be kindly disposed didn't completely offset Slocum's apprehension. In his own way, Baba was beyond Slocum's frontier of experience as much as Lucas was. At least Baba fit the classical mold of the Eastern sage, if you overlooked his red underwear and beach thongs.

Two walls later, the older man having quickly and spryly negotiated the rocky hurdles, Baba sat down abruptly on a flat yellow rock. Perched cross legged, his back perfectly erect, he smiled at Slocum and gestured to another rock two feet in front of him. Slocum folded himself down onto it and gasped for air. The Indian man wasn't out of breath at all. Maybe yogis ran a lot of wind sprints.

Baba was still silent. He watched Slocum as if he already knew he would be fascinated by what this visitor might choose to say. For a moment, Slocum was reminded of a therapist he'd seen a few times when he was trying to recuperate from a lover's betrayal.

"Well, for starters," Slocum said, "I want to thank you for seeing me on such short notice."

The yogi reached into a deep pocket and extracted a book-sized black slate. It was framed with elaborately carved sandalwood. From another pocket he produced a pencil-thin piece of white chalk. He wrote hurriedly in English script and his penmanship would've rated about a C+ in most third grade classrooms.

"This appointment was made three months ago," the slate read.

"That's odd," Slocum replied. "I just found out about it this morning. But tell me something. Why aren't you talking to me? Is this your day to observe silence or something?"

Baba smiled again, flashing his large, protruding teeth. He wiped the slate clean with the hem of his dress and scribbled, the chalk squeaking like an agitated rodent. Then he propped the board up in his lap facing Slocum, who read it aloud.

"This is my *life* to observe silence. I have not spoken in thirty-two years."

"Whoa," Slocum commented involuntarily. "Why not?" As the yogi wrote, Slocum pictured Greg in this situation. He would probably tell a knock-knock joke to try to trick Baba into forgetting himself by asking "who's there?"

"I could not control my angry tongue," the slate read. Baba erased it and wrote "How may I help you?"

"Well, Lucas suggested that you could help me make sense out of some bizarre experiences I had yesterday."

"Lucas?" the slate read.

"I'm sorry. I thought you knew each other. Lucas Dayton — big guy with a beard?"

Baba shook his head, his dark eyes radiating warmth.

"Well, anyway, let me tell you what happened."

"Go ahead," read the board.

Slocum began with the pig postcard and then described his visit to Long Marine Lab. He found himself leaving out references to Lucy's figure, how much he was attracted to her, and other unspiritual aspects of his outlook. The dolphins' sexual ecstasy was too germane to edit, though. Baba seemed to take it all in stride, listening raptly, his posture ever perfect. Slocum decided to end his tale after recounting Lucas' conversance with his recurring dream. He was conscious of consuming a lot of valuable interview time that could be spent listening.

The yogi's initial reply confused him. "There are no fireworks," the slate read.

"I don't get it," Slocum responded, cocking his head at a radical angle.

Baba wiped the slate clean and continued writing. As the board filled up and Slocum read, he repeated the process several times.

"Everything real that you can experience is matter-of-fact. If it appears otherwise, it is either not real or you are a flawed perceiver — adding your own ego as an ingredient when it does not belong there."

Slocum considered this. "But such things as I described *do* happen, right?"

"Certainly. But that is beside the point."

"What do you mean?" Slocum scrutinized the yogi's face, which was just as friendly and loving in the midst of the conversation as it had been in repose.

"It is not the happening that needs our attention. It is your *reaction* to what you *perceive* is happening. You are here talking to me. Would you be if this was just another thing that had happened?"

Slocum uncrossed his legs and ran a hand through his black curly hair. "I see your point. But isn't there some value in trying to understand unusual events?"

"Sometimes," Baba replied in his messy script. "In this instance, your ego would co-opt such information. It would be like adding aviation fuel to the gas tank of a runaway truck."

"But you don't even know me," Slocum protested. "How can you say that?"

"Unless you have purified yourself through spiritual practices, your ego is untamed. Calling it a runaway truck is a kindness; it is more like a crazy monkey."

"Maybe I *have* purified myself. How do you know?"

"It is clear that this is not a realm in which you have been expending your energy," the slate read.

"Why? Because I can't sit cross-legged forever? I don't see how you can tell."

Baba was amused at his agitation. Slocum's mind flashed back to Lucas laughing at him.

"In the moment, everything is there to be known," the yogi finally replied.

There was a silence then. Slocum was unsatisfied but couldn't seem to frame another question or remark that would catalyze the kind of answer he could use. The squeaking of Baba's chalk interrupted his frustrated cogitation.

"Let me tell you a story," the slate read. "I stole this story from the Buddhists. A young monk once sat in meditation for a long while, finally having some experiences such as you have described. Let's say he saw lights, felt energy course through him, and even had a vision." The yogi was writing and wiping about as rapidly as anyone could. "So he ran to his teacher and excitedly shared what had happened to him. The teacher patted him on the shoulder. 'Don't worry,' he said. 'Keep meditating and it will go away'."

"I think I get it," Slocum said. "I shouldn't get distracted by side-effects. Is that what you mean?"

Baba smiled again. His smile was so sweet that Slocum almost forgot what they were discussing.

"There would be little point in telling you a story," the Indian wrote, "If I then participated in reducing it to one sentence. In this situation, it is my job to tell the story, and yours to make of it what you will."

Slocum nodded. "Fair enough. But can I run something by you? I think I've got an idea here but I'm not sure about it."

Baba nodded.

"If I were a yoga student and I did everything I was supposed to do for years, this weird stuff might start happening. It would sort of be generated from within me, or at least the yoga I was doing would have something to do with it appearing. Now what I've experienced is stuff *outside* me that I haven't gradually prepared myself to deal with. So to get all involved with it would just pull me away from whatever I should be dealing with that *is* inside me."

The yogi clapped his hands together, clearly pleased by Slocum's insight.

"So to continue with that thought," Slocum said, "if you gave advice, and I don't think you do, you'd say I should meditate if I'm interested in all this. Right?"

Baba scrawled his reply. "I don't know what is right or wrong for anyone other than myself. All the answers lie within."

"So I should meditate," Slocum repeated doggedly. "That's what you're saying. That's where I'd get answers from within."

Baba threw up his hands in mock despair and then wrote, "I give up. You win. Meditate twelve hours a day. Eat only Cheerios. Buy IBM stock. Check back for further instructions every hour on the hour."

Slocum grinned as the yogi giggled noiselessly, his diaphragm bobbing up and down.

"Okay, okay," Slocum conceded. "I got a little pushy. But I'm really out of my element here. I need all the help I can get. Can I ask you specific questions — not about what I should do, but just factual stuff?"

"Sure," the slate read. The yogi was still very amused.

"What's this?" Slocum asked, holding up his right hand and wriggling his fingers in imitation of Lucas.

Baba's smile vanished. "Where did you see that?" he wrote, watching Slocum intensely as he responded.

"Lucas Dayton was doing it while he was telling me about control being an illusion."

Baba thought for a long time. "I can tell you a little bit about this." He wiped his slate with his now-dusty white hem and chose his words very carefully. "It is a complex form of mudra. Mudras are the physical manifestations of active spiritual energy. Ordinarily, they appear as customary postures or gestures. Have you ever noticed how the Buddha holds his hands when portrayed in artwork?" Slocum nodded. "These are mudras. It is the energy inside him that dictates the positions of his hands. Essentially, what you are trying to demonstrate is a less well-known form of the same phenomenon." Baba paused. "I am very concerned about what you've told me," he finally wrote. His face bore this statement out; it was almost grim. Baba's mouth was immobile and a series of vertical wrinkles had appeared between his eyes.

"Why?" Slocum asked.

"I cannot explain without betraying a confidence," the yogi replied. "It goes back fifteen years to a hut in India."

Just then a bug flew into Slocum's ear and got stuck. Buzzing wildly, it bit or stung him before managing to escape. He never saw just what it was, but Slocum's inner ear hurt like hell and he could feel it swelling already. Grimacing, he asked Baba if the event was related to their conversation. Somehow it didn't seem merely arbitrary.

"The more spiritually important the content being discussed, the more likely it is to be interrupted from the physical plane," the yogi responded.

"How about one more question?" Slocum asked, holding his ear.

"What time is it?" Baba responded.

"Five to eleven."

"One more," Baba decreed. "I have another blind date elsewhere at eleven."

"What about all these walls?" Slocum asked, gesturing at the meadow stretching before him. "Why do you people build them?"

Baba smiled mischievously and wrote, "Don't tell anyone, but I don't know!"

Eight

Slocum arrived late to the rendezvous point but his ride wasn't there yet anyway. He had walked partway up the road with Baba, enjoying the silent companionship. When the yogi had needed to veer onto another path, he had embraced Slocum with a wonderful, gut-flooding hug. It was easy to see why hundreds of people chose to live in his community. The diminutive Indian was charismatic in a down-to-earth, warm way that transcended the realm of ordinary human behavior. At least this was Slocum's point of view as he waited for Lucas. He was very impressed. And his ear hurt.

A white compact car pulled up. Lucy was driving.

"Hop in," she called through the open passenger side window.

So he did. Lucy performed an impeccable K-turn and headed back towards town.

"How'd it go?" she asked.

"Great."

"Did he answer all your questions?" Lucy glanced at Slocum and some aspect of her expression implied that she already knew how he would reply.

"Well, no. But I feel a lot better about things. Where's Lucas anyway?"

"He had something he had to do."

"Don't you have to work today?" Slocum asked.

"Nope."

Lucy wore khaki shorts with cuffs, a faded red tee shirt, and light brown Birkenstock sandals. Her golden hair was pulled back into a ponytail, secured with a red piece of yarn. Her long legs were very tan and fit; Slocum watched them work the pedals as she adeptly shifted from fourth to third gear to negotiate a curve.

"So you liked Baba?" Lucy asked.

"What's not to like? I can't imagine anyone disliking him."

"How about all the families of people he's brainwashed?"

"You're joking, right?"

"No. That's *their* perspective. A crazy old Indian man has transformed their child or sister or whatever into some kind of religious fanatic or astro-zombie."

"But it's not like he's Jim Jones or Reverend Moon or something."

"Hey, *we* know that. But believe me, there're plenty of people that don't like him. Other spiritual leaders are jealous of his success too. It's a pretty competitive scene out there."

"Really? That seems so odd." Slocum rubbed his sore ear too roughly and winced.

"You've just been lucky. Normally you have to sift through a whole bunch of half-assed situations before you meet someone like Lucas or Baba Ahimsa."

"I wasn't even looking."

"That's true. You're on a charmed path, Slocum. I envy you."

This struck Slocum as an intriguing way to reframe his circumstances. Here he was, thrust into an unfamiliar context that was littered with scary occult phenomena, and was apparently populated by extraordinary beings who made him feel like a four year old. And the most beautiful creature he'd happened upon in this transcendent realm wanted to change places with him. Go figure.

"I'm not sure I want to be on a path at all," he confessed. The car began the long descent into the Pajaro Valley.

"It's not an optional thing," Lucy replied. "We're all on our own unique paths. Some people are conscious of it and some aren't, that's all."

"Hitler was on a spiritual path?"

"Of course. These things don't make sense when they're taken out of context, Slocum. You have to factor karma into it and realize that we reincarnate millions of times."

"I don't know much about your point of view," Slocum admitted. "I mean I've read about it, but put yourself in my place. Do you remember when you encountered all this Eastern philosophy firsthand?"

Lucy shook her head, her ponytail whipping back and forth. "It was different for me. When I was a kid, I was tuned in to this. I used to go sit in the woods and feel the energy. I had visions too."

"Don't worry," Slocum told her. "If you keep sitting, they'll go away."

Lucy looked at him curiously. "That's exactly what happened. I don't know where you come up with this stuff."

Slocum smiled enigmatically.

"Anyway," Lucy continued, "when I stumbled onto Eastern religions, it was all familiar — it resonated with what I knew as a kid. So our paths are too different to compare, really."

"Okay, fine. But here's my point. I didn't sign up anywhere. I'm not a seeker. I'm not religious. I study the *history* of consciousness, and in my case this has consisted of what's starting to look like a whole lot of intellectual bullshit. Now, in the last twenty-four hours I've experienced a lot of heavy-duty genuine shit. It takes all my resources to cope. So there's nothing left that can 'take karma into account' and all that."

"I understand. Sorry. This is just very exciting and I forget. It doesn't happen this way very often, Slocum. You're really special. The universe is probably preparing you for some major mission."

"Say what?"

"Never mind. I was doing it again. Sorry." She noticed him fiddling with his ear. "What's the matter with your ear?"

"A bug flew into it and stung me. It hurts like hell. It's swollen and it's pulsing and I don't like it."

"No wonder you're so cranky, she commented.

"I'm not cranky. I'm just..."

"Cranky."

"Tired," he finished.

"Cranky."

"Maybe 'saturated.'"

"Cranky."

"*Now* I'm cranky."

"See? I told you so."

Slocum smiled in spite of himself. "You're so immature," he said.

"Am *not!*" she proclaimed shrilly, sticking out her very pink tongue.

* * *

Back at the Town Clock after another half hour of thinly disguised flirting, Lucy relinquished her passenger and promised to stay in touch. Slocum retrieved his bike and set off for home, but he hadn't pedaled more than a couple of revolutions when a fierce-looking homeless man stepped in front of him and held up his hands. Slocum grabbed his brakes and screeched to a stop.

The man was short and thin and feral. His fierceness was projected by his cocky body language and a very hard, defiant expression, especially in the eyes. He wore a blue and black flannel shirt and olive-green fatigue pants. His hair was brown, long, and matted. Dark stubble covered old burn scars on his chin and left cheek. He was probably in his mid-forties, and was by no means Slocum's first pick of who he'd like to be hustled by.

"I haven't got any spare change," he told the man.

"Just listen up, buddy. You tell your friend to keep away from here. If he lays another hand on Junior, he's a dead man." The words were stated flatly, without affect. His voice was rough and uneducated, with a smoker's burr.

"I think you've got me mixed up with someone else," Slocum managed to say.

The man crooked a finger, at someone standing in Slocum's peripheral vision, and the schizophrenic leg-hugger stumbled over and stood behind him.

"This is Junior. You tell your friend what I said."

"Sure. Okay."

The man strode forward and stepped right in Slocum's face, standing much closer than social mores allowed. When he winked, Slocum flinched and drew back involuntarily.

"They call me Flinch," the man told him, grinning. His teeth were a mess.

"I can see why," Slocum responded, mustering a weak grin of his own.

"You want some advice?" Flinch asked.

"Sure." As long as this guy was going to stand six inches away, Slocum was going to be agreeable.

"You stay away from your friend too. That is one bad-ass dude, man. I'm not bullshitting you. I know what I'm talking about."

"Hey thanks. Look, I've gotta go."

Flinch stepped aside. "So go, man."

"Right." Slocum sped away, his legs pumping in response to the adrenalin flowing in him.

"*Jesus*," he thought. "What next?"

Nine

After a long nap, replete with soothing dreams, Slocum telephoned Greg and asked him over for lunch.

"Bring the lunch," he added. "I'll provide one of the mouths."

"Gee, that sounds fair."

"I'll make it worth your while."

"You'd better."

While he waited for Greg, Slocum slouched on his loveseat and read a journal article for his class on nineteenth-century European politics. It was amazing how the author managed to filter exciting ideas through his ax-grinding viewpoint, producing a thin, gray, boring, intellectual gruel. So many of the articles Slocum read sought to narrow the reader's perspective until it matched the groove the author had settled into. What nurtured him were the occasional gems that opened him up more, that gave him glimpses of how things *might* be. These actually informed, or even catalyzed insights, as opposed to merely conniving to convince.

Greg was a militant about pedants. If he was forced to read anything he deemed "written by the undead", he lampooned it mercilessly. Many professors failed to appreciate this facet of their student's personality. He only got away with it by virtue of his brilliance in other classroom endeavors.

The front door banged open and Greg burst in, a grocery bag under one arm.

"Where is she?" he brayed.

"Who?"

"She Who Will Make It Worth My While. I will accept no less."

"In that case, she's in the bathroom. She'll be right out," Slocum replied. "What's for lunch?"

"Sandwiches."

"What kind of sandwiches?"

"Yummy sandwiches."

"Oh good. My favorite."

Greg lay on the floor next to Slocum's horrendously ugly brown plastic coffee table and began flourishing wrapped packages.

"They're lovely," Slocum commented. "It's like Christmas."

"That's just the kind of profound remark that can't replace a naked woman for making something worth someone's while," Greg told him.

"Amen to that," Slocum responded. "I'm sure she'll be out of the bathroom in a minute."

The living room felt crowded with six foot four inch Greg sprawled in it. Technically, several more people could've squeezed into the space, but they would have had to be either close acquaintances or proponents of the Flinch handbook of social etiquette.

Greg wore purple nylon gym shorts, old Converse basketball shoes, and a dingy white tee shirt featuring an array of little black armadillos drinking Lone Star Beer on it. In college, Greg had tried to keep a pet armadillo in his dorm room, but it had died so he'd placed it in the salad bar at the student center. This initiated a long series of copycat pranks, which introduced such unlikely salad items as bowling balls, hamsters, and Barbie dolls into the University of Texas food chain.

As usual, Greg's hair and beard sported the wind tunnel look so popular among those chic few who didn't have mirrors in their houses. His bushy blond beard was especially shapeless that day. One side sort of resembled ranks of parallel upside-down obelisks; the other side was beyond analogy.

The sandwiches were turkey and jack cheese on french rolls with lots of hot mustard. They ate voraciously, swigging Mexican beer between mouthfuls.

Many crumbs were created; none were tidily retrieved by the meal's participants.

"That hit the spot," Slocum proclaimed after finishing.

"Yup," Greg agreed, sitting up and brushing his mustache with the back of his hand. This served to relocate those crumbs above his lip to the hairy purgatory below his chin. "So what's the deal? What happened yesterday with the freak pig postcard?"

"God, was it only yesterday? Well, let's see. I think I met Ms. Right, I made dolphins act weird, and I met two gurus. Did I leave anything out? Oh yeah, I was threatened by a street guy, I've had bizarre physical symptoms, and a bee or something flew in my ear and stung me."

"That's it?"

"Well, I'm leaving out a few details like one of the gurus knowing my dreams and doing mudras, and the woman thinking I'm the second coming or something."

"I take it you don't mean that in its sexual sense?"

"No, in the messianic sense. Your basic major mission on Earth, et cetera."

"Hmmm. Does she have a sister?"

"I don't know."

"What's a mudra?"

"I gather it's like a hand gesture that happens when energy zips around in your body," Slocum told him.

"Like when your leg twitches as you're falling asleep?"

"I don't think so, but what do I know?"

"Was DeGrazia one of the gurus?"

"How'd you remember that? No, she doesn't even work at the marine lab anymore. Lucy does, though."

"Lucy is Ms. Right?"

Slocum nodded.

"So why'd she send the postcard?"

"She didn't. She didn't know anything about it."

"So you don't either?"

"Uh-uh. But I don't care. I've got too much else going on."

"Why don't you tell me the whole thing step by step?"

"Sure." Slocum slouched in the loveseat and methodically recounted his tale. Greg received the unvarnished, complete version, biased only by selective memory, skewed

perceptions, and the like. The percentage of actual reality that
was represented was probably about average.

"Are you interested in feedback?" Greg asked Slocum
when he'd concluded.

"Absolutely. Let 'er rip."

"Well, several things jumped out at me. First of all, the
dolphins jumping up and only splashing certain people strikes
me as no big deal. They're smart and they're playful, so that's
the kind of thing they do, I think. Now the orgasm thing is
different. That is *way* weird, no two ways about it. Could Lucy
just be lying about what their noises meant?"

"Why would she? And if she did, she's the best actress I
ever saw. Hell, she blushed about it. And then there's the fact
that I'm so attracted to her. I've never fallen for any big liars
before."

"Okay, okay. I was just asking. Another thing that struck
me was the way that both Lucas and Baba — God I feel silly
saying that name — were charismatic, but in different ways.
Lucas sounds like an authority figure — some guy that knows
things he won't tell. He holds onto his power, you know what I
mean? And even though Baba didn't really tell you anything
either, he comes across as this totally different kind of guy —
sort of an Eastern Santa Claus."

"Yeah, that's true."

Greg rubbed his forehead and frowned. "I've got
something else to say that I'm real embarrassed about. It's
about this white farmhouse dream thing."

"Yeah?"

"Well, you know I'm in this dream interpretation group,
right?"

"Don't tell me. You told them *my* dream."

"Not exactly. I tell my real dreams in the group, even
though they've been pretty boring lately. But there's this one
really beautiful girl in there and sometimes we go out for
coffee."

"Is she a blonde with green eyes?"

"No. She's got short brown hair and brown eyes. Her
name's Nancy and I told her a few of your dreams once a few
months ago. You know how interesting some of yours are — I

was just trying to impress her. Now I can't imagine that this is where Lucas got hold of your dream, but I felt like I needed to tell you anyway."

"That's a pretty sleazy thing to do. Did it work?"

"No."

"Bummer."

"No shit. So I'm sorry now I did it — not just because I didn't get anywhere with Nancy. Do *you* think that's how Lucas knew your dream?"

"It seems pretty unlikely. It was a while ago and it wasn't such a big deal that your friend would naturally go blabbing all around about it. And his knowing is consistent with the rest of Lucas — his presence and the other things he knows." Slocum paused and stared up and to his left. "You know, a couple of days ago I'd have picked any normal explanation over any abnormal one. But something's shifted. Now, I don't know."

"Don't know what?"

Slocum cocked his head in a characteristic manner. "I don't even know what I don't know. It feels like everything's up for grabs."

"Is that good?"

"I don't know. It's different. It's like there's unlimited potential, but it's unsettling too. I guess if I took it real seriously, I'd have to have a big reaction, but I'm just kind of going along and seeing what happens."

"Hell, that's a good way to go through life anyway."

"Yeah. I guess so." Slocum didn't sound too convinced.

"Can I get a job doing P.R. or something if you become Christ?"

"Okay."

"How about book rights? Can I write the authorized biography?"

"If you're good."

"Oh boy."

"I see you're adopting your usual serious attitude, Greg."

"Hey, even if this is all true, it's still ridiculous. I don't mean because you're such an improbable candidate. I mean in the sense that all life is absurd. If I took *anything* seriously, I'd be a basket case. That's just the way I am."

"Aren't there some things that force you to get serious? Suppose your mother died?"

"Well, I don't know for sure because it hasn't happened and maybe I'd feel different if it really did, but I picture myself feeling sad and grieving like anyone else. But I don't equate 'sad' with 'serious.'"

"I can't see you cracking jokes about her at the funeral."

"Of course not. Being 'not serious' isn't the same as being comical either. I'd think of her death as another ridiculous event — something I'll never understand, something nonsensical. That's what makes life unserious — the fact that the significance of everything is forever beyond my reach. The true nature of reality may be serious, or silly, or *whatever* — I'll never know. So I've picked 'absurd' as my way to cope since that's what it usually *seems* like."

"I get what you're saying," Slocum responded. "I think we're just different about this. I have a sense that things do fit together somehow. I don't know how and I probably never will, but it would only be absurd to me if life was random, and I just feel way down in my gut that it isn't."

"That's why you get to be Christ and I have to stay home, mind the kids, scrub the floors, work my fingers to the bone.... But I'll be fine. You just go off and save the world, honey."

Slocum shook his head. "You're a walking advertisement for your point of view, Greg."

"Thanks. I think you're swell too."

Ten

After Greg took off to the library, Slocum resumed his reading and prepared a presentation for his seminar in German philosophy. He didn't understand the arbitrary groupings the university used in creating graduate level classes. Why glop together philosophers by nationality? Surely their ideas transcended geographical borders? Why not group them by similarity of point of view or even the eras they lived in? One professor had explained to Slocum that the ideas of great thinkers arose from specific traditions and must be understood in that context. But more frequently Slocum sensed connections that spanned cultures, such as the similarities between Confucius and Italian Renaissance thought. Lately he'd been considering basing his thesis on some premise such as this, but he knew he'd get flak for it.

Slocum worked diligently the rest of the daylight hours. After a dinner of chicken pot pie and frozen broccoli, he received a series of significant phone calls. The first one was from Lucas.

"Was your visit to Cruz Mountain satisfying?" the older man asked.

"Satisfying? Hmm... I don't know. In terms of getting answers, Baba's just about as frustrating as you are. But I really enjoyed meeting him."

"Great. Would you have an interest in meeting Saddhu Ramba?"

"The sixties guy? Carl Goldberg?"

"Yes."

"I thought he lived up in Marin County."

"He's visiting friends in Santa Cruz.

"How can you arrange all this?"

"It's nothing. Just give me the word if you're interested."

"Well, sure. I've read all his books. Why would he want to see me?"

"Until you understand who you are, you can't know the answer to that."

"He doesn't still advocate that everyone take LSD, does he?"

Lucas' laughter boomed through the phone line. "No, no. He's strictly a spiritual fellow these days — kind of a guru to the New Age folks. He gives talks, works for charity — he's service oriented, that's the best way to put it."

"But he knows about energy and all that?"

"Absolutely. Years ago in India, Saddhu Ramba was very involved in these matters. He was a disciple of Brahmachari's, you know."

"Who?"

"The guru of gurus. Brahmachari. You probably know him as the man who is supposed to have said 'just live and you'll love.' There was a very popular song a few years ago in which this phrase was repeated over and over."

"I remember the song, but I don't think I've ever heard of Brahmachari."

"That's not surprising. He died twelve years ago, he wrote very little, and he didn't speak. Also he took great pains to ensure that no organization grew around him. But indirectly he's been responsible for most of the spiritual progress in this century."

"I'll bet your fingers are going a mile a minute. Am I right?"

"Right you are, my friend. And someday I'll tell you all about that."

"Did Brahmachari do mudras too?"

"As a matter of fact, he did. Where did you run across that word?"

"Baba Ahimsa mentioned it."

"Ah, I see. Much of Brahmachari's work was universal in nature. That is, he worked with energy on other planes more than he helped individuals. So mudras were instrumental to him. But that's enough. I have my own work to do and I'm sure you do too. Be at the lighthouse on West Cliff at nine tomorrow morning. Saddhu Ramba will meet you there."

"Okay. Thanks."

"Goodbye, Slocum."

"Bye."

The phone chirped again almost immediately.

"Hello?"

"Is this Slocum Happler?" an unfamiliar man's voice asked in clipped tones.

"Yes."

"I'm Detective Perry of the Santa Cruz police department. Do you have a few minutes?"

"Sure. How can I help you?"

"Well it appears that you were the last person to see Baba Ahimsa alive. Is that true?"

"*What?*"

"Mr. Ahimsa died around 11:15 this morning. It appears that he suffered a cerebral hemorrhage. He *was* in his eighties, I'm told. Your name came up so I'm just double-checking to see if he acted odd or said anything about how he was feeling."

"I can't believe it. He's dead? He was fine when I saw him. Better than fine — he was totally alive."

"So you didn't notice anything unusual?"

"God. I don't know. I mean he was an unusual man. But I only met him today. I wouldn't know what was usual or unusual, really."

"I see. And what was the nature of your appointment?"

"Uh, gee, I guess you could say I was getting spiritual counseling."

"I see," the detective responded neutrally. "Now there is one twist to this, and that's that the Cruz Mountain people were apparently led to believe that their leader would tell them some special thing before he died. He also said he'd let them know ahead of time when he would die, but I'm not too concerned about that. With a massive brain hemorrhage, you're gone in seconds. Anyway, you may be hearing from those people. Is that a problem?"

"No, that's fine."

"Right. Well, then, thanks for your cooperation."

"No problem."

"Good night."

Slocum was stunned. Without a policeman's questions to distract him from his feelings, he was flooded with undifferentiated emotion. He didn't know exactly what he felt, but he knew he was feeling a great deal of *something*. His solar plexus was clenched and hot. His face was flushed and his teeth hurt.

The phone chirped again, derailing his train of thought.

"Yes?"

"Hello. Is this Slocum Happler?" It was another unfamiliar voice, this time a woman's.

"Maybe," he answered.

"This is Essa Pearlhut from the Cruz Mountain Yoga Center."

"Okay, yeah, I'm me."

"Have you heard about Baba?"

"Yes. Just now. I'm very upset."

"You saw him this morning?"

"Yes. He was fine."

"Did he say anything about the walls?"

"Huh?"

"The walls we build. We know they're important and Baba told us he'd tell us about them before he dropped his body. Since you happened to be the last person he communicated with, some of us think he must've revealed the answer to you."

"Well, this is very awkward. I actually did ask him — his answer was the last thing he wrote. But he asked me not to tell anyone what it was."

There was an intake of breath on the line. Then the woman spoke in an urgent, serious tone. "Mr. Happler, you have no idea how important this is to us. It may be the only thing that can keep the community together now. It's no coincidence that the secret of the walls was the last thing he wrote before he dropped his body. We *need* to know. Surely you can see that."

"I'm sorry. He was very generous with me and this was the only thing he asked in return — not to tell what he said. I just can't."

There was a long pause. "Who *are* you?" the woman finally asked.

"What do you mean?"

"Why you? Why have you suddenly shown up and assumed this key role in our lives? Are you a yogi? No one here knows you. Who *are* you?"

"I'm just a graduate student from Texas. That's all. Just another person bumbling through life, really."

"Why did you see Baba?"

"Well, some unusual things have been happening lately and a friend who knows more about these things thought that Baba could help me understand them."

"Ah, there *is* something special about you."

"No, really. Baba told me not to pay attention to all that."

"All what?"

"Look, lady. I'm not special and I can't help you. I'm sorry. About that and about Baba dying. I'm *really* sorry about that. I've never met anyone like him and I'm sure everyone up there is pretty torn up about it. But I'm not playing any key role in anything. Honest."

There was another long pause. "Thank you for your time, Mr. Happler," she mumbled woodenly.

"You're welcome. Hang in there."

"Goodbye."

Slocum hung up and lay on his back on the rug in front on the loveseat. The spackle on the ceiling's sheetrock made patterns if you squinted real hard. Slocum squinted real hard. Eventually he fell asleep on the floor.

Eleven

At eight-fifty the following morning, Slocum sat on the steps of the brick lighthouse on West Cliff Drive. It wasn't a towering pillar shining its mighty fog-cutting beam miles into Monterey Bay. It had been funded by a grieving mother in memorial to a son who had surfed onto the rocks below the point of land it stood on. The lighthouse was perhaps one-sixth in scale, and although a weak light swept across the adjacent waters, no one used it for navigation. A few years earlier, the one-room interior had been converted into a surfing museum, replete with obsolete longboards and photographs of early competitions at Steamer's Lane, a famous surf spot just down the coast from the lighthouse. Directly seaward was deep water and then Seal Rock, home to thirty or forty sea lions, who packed the rugged surface like a chubby jigsaw puzzle.

The lighthouse was a popular meeting place for walkers and bicyclists setting out on the clifftop asphalt path that paralleled West Cliff Drive all the way up to Natural Bridges State Park.

It was cool and overcast on this particular Friday morning; Slocum wished he'd worn more than just his sweatshirt. Part of the problem was that he was just sitting. Had he been one of the joggers or brisk walkers that were streaming past him, he'd have been fine.

A few dozen yards away the surf pounded a complex rhythm, churning up rich oceanic odors. Slocum would've expected to hear the waves more than he smelled them, but the distance from the water successfully muted the aggregation of sounds. As he drew in a robust snootful of marine air, Slocum spied Saddhu Ramba across the parking lot.

The former Princeton professor was now in his sixties and looked it. He was nearly bald, with just a few wisps of white hair encircling his gleaming pink pate. He wore brightly colored clothes, stood about five foot nine, and was slightly overweight. As he drew closer, Slocum could discern a vast network of lines, wrinkles, and fissures that overlaid Saddhu's features. Closer yet and the man's eyes dominated his visage. They were pale blue, soft and very present. It was as if he lived in his eyes, way out on the periphery of his being, instead of hiding inside somewhere. There was nothing scary about the phenomenon; the being who approached Slocum exuded warmth and good cheer. Under a gray and white mustache, Saddhu Ramba smiled expansively as he caught Slocum's eye.

"Good morning," he called.

"Good morning," Slocum replied, rising and offering his hand. "I'm Slocum Happler."

Saddhu ignored his hand and embraced him in a bear hug. At first, Slocum stiffened, resenting the encroachment. Then he relaxed and yielded to the sensation of being held by someone who loved him. It was odd how obvious that fact was. The hug was so clearly an expression of love that every part of Saddhu that was touching him seemed to communicate it.

When the older man released him and stepped back, Slocum was nonplussed.

"I'm a pretty good hugger, aren't I?" Saddhu said. His voice was gentle but strong, with a slight New York accent.

Slocum nodded.

"We're all in this together," Saddhu told him. Slocum recognized this phrase as the title of one of Saddhu's books, but in the moment the remark came across as fresh — an apt commentary on hugging, loving, and why they were even standing there by the lighthouse.

"Shall we walk?" Saddhu suggested.

Slocum nodded again. Once they were moving, his brain and tongue reconnected. "Thanks for meeting me," he said.

The twosome strode side by side a few yards on the wide path before Saddhu replied. "When Marcus Beecham needs a favor, I'm there. We go back a long way."

"Is that who contacted you?"

"Yes, although it wouldn't surprise me if you knew him by another name. Marcus can be quite a rascal."

Slocum recognized that for Saddhu this label represented one of his more pejorative evaluations. Mass murderers were probably "scamps" to the man. Slocum was reminded of a story that his Texan uncle loved to tell, and insisted was true. A man walks into a bar, and gets into a couple of arguments, so he whips out a pistol and starts shooting. When the smoke clears, as the man gets hauled off by the police, an old black man turns to Slocum's uncle and says "Moody little feller, ain't he?"

"Is Marcus tall with long hair and a big multi-colored beard?" Slocum asked as they passed an elderly couple with matching black canes.

"That's him. We studied under the same master in India."

Slocum absorbed this fact as he gazed over the cliff at the ocean. While he pondered the implications, some part of him noticed that the odors had changed. It was fishier and riper smelling now, almost cloying. Then something clicked into place in Slocum's mind.

"You, Lucas — I mean Marcus — and Baba Ahimsa were all with Brahmachari in India about fifteen years ago, right?"

"Along with a few others as well. That's right." Saddhu smiled and nodded. "In fact, there's a man in town named Feng Shi who's just as unlikely a guru as Marcus. The two of them were always getting into trouble even in India."

"I just realized something. You probably don't know about Baba yet."

"Know what?" Saddhu's beautiful eyes narrowed.

"He died yesterday morning. Cerebral hemorrhage."

"Oh my." The older man's face spoke more forcefully than his words.

"I was the last person to see him alive, apparently."

Saddhu was silent. They walked for half a block before he spoke again. "Did he explain the walls to anyone before he died?"

"Yeah. Me."

"Well don't keep me in suspense."

"He asked me not to tell anyone," Slocum explained.

Saddhu burst into warm laughter. "Oh, that's perfect. That's Baba!" He halted on the walkway to hold his ribs as he laughed. "I'm sure going to miss him," he finally said. Noticing Slocum's confused reaction to his odd style of mourning, he added, "Death gets a lot of bad press in this country, but actually it's perfectly safe."

"I'll have to think about that."

They resumed walking and dodged a bevy of roller skaters.

"It's beautiful here, isn't it?" Saddhu asked.

Slocum wasn't sure if he meant West Cliff or the planet Earth but in either case he agreed, so he nodded. "It sure is."

The sun was just beginning to break through behind them, casting long shadows and enticing the scrubby vegetation into glowing and crowning the top of the cliffs with an unaccustomed majesty. For a second, Slocum saw everything in focus — foreground, background, even peripheral vision. It was one of those moments when the light and a certain attitude combine to enhance one's visual input in all sorts of ways. The trees across the street in Lighthouse Field seemed to be more three dimensional than usual. Everywhere Slocum looked, subtle hues separated themselves so that each object was a compendium of color. And the water elegantly revealed what was under its surface with ever-shifting clues that Slocum could read without effort. Maybe painters saw the world this way all the time, but it was a precious moment for him. The spell broke when Saddhu spoke again; the world returned to merely being beautiful.

"How may I help you?" he asked.

"I'm not sure. A lot of strange, intense things have been happening lately. I don't know whether to talk about Lucas not being Lucas, the Baba's last words business, or the dolphins that have orgasms when I touch them. I mean, where do I even start?"

"If you're concerned about your master no longer being in his body, don't be. My guru has been dead for over a decade, but he's always here with me," he said, tapping his heart.

"I only met Baba yesterday," Slocum told him. "I don't have a guru, unless you count Lucas — I mean Marcus."

"How long have you known him?" Saddhu asked.

"Two days. Two crazy days."

"Perhaps Marcus should be the subject of our talk, then. He is a most unusual soul."

"Amen to that."

"He is both an advanced spiritual being and an unbalanced one. He embodies all facets of humankind at the same time that he transcends them. It's very hard to explain. Marcus is the most complex individual I've ever met."

"Is he really an anesthesiologist?"

"Is that what he told you? No, he's an ear, nose and throat specialist — or he used to be. I wonder why he misrepresented something so trivial? He does everything for a reason. Make no mistake about that. His reasons may not be comprehensible to you, but to him they flow from the choreography that the universe has expressed."

"Choreography?"

"He didn't mention that? That's the cornerstone of his philosophy. He's been trying to publish "How To Read God's Choreography" for years. The idea is that if you can totally go with the flow, God shows you what to do. It's like being a dancer. The choreography shows you the outline of the composition, but then you dance your own steps within that structure. It's really a useful metaphor."

"Then why can't he get it published?"

"Marcus is an extremist. He pits his ideas against everyone else's and I think publishers shy away from that. On the one hand, he presents beautiful theological ideas, but on the other hand his presentation itself is aggressive. I doubt if too many people can reconcile these things."

"Is he dangerous? Should I be involved with him?"

"You're the only one that can answer that. It's possible to learn a great deal from even a lunatic, let alone Marcus. Alternately, you can become lost in someone else's delusions. There's a French word for that — it's an actual category in mental health."

"I'm getting pretty concerned," Slocum told him. "I don't need to be involved with a nut. Life is hard enough anyway."

"How involved are you?" Saddhu asked as he gestured for them to turn around and begin retracing their steps. "Why don't you tell me how you met him and what's happened so far?"

"Sure." For what seemed like the hundredth time, Slocum told his story. Saddhu Ramba listened carefully, occasionally nodding or smiling at people they passed on the path. Slocum's soliloquy consumed a good half of the return trip, followed by a lengthy silence.

"Don't worry about the parlor tricks," Saddhu finally began. "They're not important. All they do is tell you that the people and the situation are not ordinary, which we already know. You can be crazy and psychic, or selfish and charismatic. Parlor tricks are by no means exclusive to saints." A cloud skidded in front of the sun as they strode by a bicyclist repairing her chain. "If I were you, I'd try to verify everything that has seemed to happen. Marcus is a maestro with illusion. He knows how to work with it. Who knows how much of what you've experienced is real? I don't." Saddhu seemed to be picking up the pace of their stroll as he spoke. Slocum struggled to keep up. "The main thing, though, is to follow your heart. If Marcus suggests you do something that your inner teacher tells you is wrong, then don't do it. Everyone has an inner teacher that lives in their heart. Just learn to listen — to differentiate that voice from all the others. That's your best guide in any situation."

"Thank you. That makes a lot of sense to me," Slocum replied.

"Let me give you my phone number too. If something comes up that you want to discuss with me, it would be fine to call me."

"Great."

"And don't go see Feng Shi if Marcus suggests it. That could be dangerous," Saddhu counseled.

They were almost back at the diminutive lighthouse. A tourist family was arranging itself on the steps for a group photo. An elderly man with a rambunctious Airedale puppy had been solicited to be the photographer, but the leashed pup kept pulling him off balance. Saddhu Ramba stepped forward and offered to hold the dog while the portrait was being snapped. It was the sort of thing that never occurred to Slocum, yet was clearly what the situation called for.

Slocum and Saddhu parted company after another superlative hug. As the Texan pulled out of the parking lot, the sun peeked out for just a second, flashing on Saddhu Ramba's bare scalp as he stepped onto a path that meandered through Lighthouse Field. Then the illumination was shielded once more and the older man disappeared from view, lost in the tall weeds and the gray morning haze.

Twelve

After his early afternoon class Slocum decided to follow Saddhu's advice and confirm a few of the particulars he had encountered. He meandered down to the pay phones at McHenry Library to call Long Marine Lab, since Lucy seemed to be his best source on Lucas/Marcus.

"Hello. Long Marine Lab. This is Julie. How can I help you?" Julie's voice was very high and pure, like a sixties folksinger.

"Hello. Could I speak to Lucy Griffin, please?"

"Just a moment." It was a long moment. "I'm sorry. There's no one by that name that works here."

"Oh. Well is there someone that works with the dolphins I could talk to?"

"There's the trainer — Sue Tuggle — and then there's some researchers. What does this pertain to?"

"Uh, it would be really hard to explain, but if I could talk to Sue for five minutes I think that would do it."

"I'll see if she's back from lunch." There was a click.

Slocum glanced at his watch, which read ten after three. If the real trainer took such a late lunch, then he may have met Lucy while the trainer was away. He didn't understand why, but it was beginning to look like the whole thing was some kind of hoax. Slocum felt light-headed and his stomach hurt. He was suddenly aware of a peculiar smell emanating from the telephone receiver. It was a cross between bananas and hair spray which struck him as being an extremely unlikely combination.

"Hello? This is Sue. What can I do for you?" Her voice was nothing like Lucy's.

"Hi. My name is Slocum Happler and I *really* need to ask you a few questions. Have you got a minute?"

"Sure." Sue sounded like a nice person.

"Do the dolphins ever jump out of the water and just splash certain people?"

"They sure do. That's one of their favorite tricks."

"Are you usually at lunch around two o'clock?"

"Yes. What's this about?"

"I'll tell you in a minute but I've got to ask something else first. When people pet the dolphins, do they make this real unearthly sound?"

"Yes."

"And this is kind of embarrassing, but is that like the sound they make when they have sex?"

"Where did you ever get that idea? They don't sound anything like that when they're mating. And they won't mate when they're living in a pool this small, anyway. Now what's this all about?"

"Somebody seems to have played a practical joke on me while you were on your lunch hour."

"Oh. I see." Sue didn't seem to know what to say.

"Can I ask one last thing?"

"Go ahead."

"How did you guys get the pool so round?"

"You're kidding, right? It isn't round at all. There are thousands of angles built into the side walls so the dolphins can navigate with their sonar. If it was round, they'd be smashing into the side all the time. Are you sure you were here at the lab? Could your friend have tricked you about where you were?"

"No, that's the one thing I wasn't an idiot about. Thanks for your help."

"Sure. I've got to run. Good luck."

"Bye bye."

Well, well, well. It was all a crock. An elaborate, well-planned crock. If Marcus and whoever Lucy really was could fabricate reality at that level, they could easily have managed to get a hold of his dream through Greg, and God knows what else. Maybe Lucy had donned a wig and contact lenses to beguile his buddy. Hell, she could blush on command. She was obviously a talented actress and a whiz at improvisation.

But why go to all that trouble? Slocum didn't have any money or anything else anybody would want. And surely no guru was so hard up for followers; there must be plenty of seekers out there only too happy to sign up with someone as impressive as Marcus. Anyway, how long could anyone keep up a deception so rooted in lies? They must've known that Saddhu Ramba would blow their cover.

No matter what motive Slocum could imagine, the hoax seemed like overkill as a means to an end. That was the main thing. Could some people just enjoy the process of fooling other people? Slocum remembered Saddhu's comment on Marcus: he always had reasons for what he did, even if they weren't comprehensible.

Slocum gathered his notebooks and left McHenry Library. As soon as he exited, though, he once again felt a need to think things over. He sprawled on a flat wooden bench, propping his schoolwork under his head. As he gazed up at a patch of blue sky between several redwoods, his mind wandered.

At least he'd met two great men. And even if he hadn't consciously understood everything Baba Ahimsa or Saddhu Ramba had said, surely he'd absorbed a portion of the wisdom on some level. It couldn't hurt anyway. And he had really enjoyed dinner with Lucy, even if now it turned out to be based on crap. She was one of the prettiest women he'd ever met; it had been exciting to hang out with her.

On the other hand, he had definitely attained major chumphood; he had been thoroughly humiliated. While he hadn't entirely bought the "you're so special" routine, it had hooked him enough to keep him totally manipulated. Probably Marcus and Lucy were laughing their brains out at his expense. Well, actually, that didn't sound like them. But they'd have the right to if they felt like it.

"Hi Slocum," Garnet called. She was a sixty-eight year old fellow graduate student.

He sat up. "Hi Garnet. How's it going with the clowns?" Her thesis detailed the evolution of clowning as a cause of World War I.

She was a visor person and wore a purple one, along with all sorts of mismatched clothes. Slocum liked her a lot.

"I can see it's going better for me than for you," Garnet replied, studying his face.

"Have you ever felt like a total fool?" he asked.

"Of course." She sat down next to him and patted him on the arm. Garnet was about five feet tall and her tiny legs dangled off the bench. She was wearing bright green fishnet stockings.

"Hey, I like your stockings," Slocum said.

"No you don't. You think they're way too flashy for a woman my age."

"Maybe I do," he admitted.

"That's okay. I don't mind. And don't worry. There are times when everybody plays the fool." She hopped up. "I've got a study date."

"Is he single, Garnet?"

"Of course." She bustled off, her long white braid swinging like a tail. She was a relentless flirt who never missed an opportunity to commune with younger men.

Slocum's second stab at leaving for his remaining class was more successful than the first, although he never did actually enter the classroom. On the front steps of the building he decided to head home and take a long escape-from-life nap. He felt he richly deserved it, and Professor Tice was a tyrant with less than fully focused students. Once he'd climbed onto the oval seminar table and kicked everyone's books into their laps, which proved to be rather painful for several of the male students. Greg had distributed a leaflet before the next session advertising the "Tice Memorial protective cup" for $7.99. When their professor found one of the fliers, he laughed uproariously and then assigned four hundred pages of reading for the next class.

*   *   *

At his front door Slocum was hailed by a male voice from the sidewalk.

"Slocum Happler?"

He turned and appraised the two fortyish men who stood in front of a new blue Chevy sedan.

One was black, a lean well-dressed man with an air of authority. The way he stood implied movement; perhaps he had been an athlete. His expression was friendly but Slocum sensed that something serious was motivating him.

The other man was slightly older and shorter. He wore a bedraggled wide-wale tan corduroy jacket and black dress slacks, which were a bit too long. His broad face seemed puzzled, as though it could muster emotions independently of the rest of him. His eyes were remarkably small and deep set. He could've been Hispanic or perhaps he was just very tan. All in all, he had the air of a Labrador Retriever who was waiting for someone to throw his ball.

"I'm Slocum," Slocum told them.

The men strode forward, the black man first.

"I'm Detective Perry and this is Sergeant Morino."

Slocum held out his hand as the men approached. "We spoke on the phone."

"That's right," Perry replied, shaking his hand firmly and smiling affably. He moved aside; Sergeant Morino took Slocum's hand as well and nodded impersonally.

"We need to ask you a few questions," the black man told Slocum.

"Come on in." He pushed open the unlocked front door, maneuvered through the living room, and plopped down onto the one chair, leaving the green loveseat for the policemen. They squeezed into it after standing a moment and glancing around the tiny house.

"I hope neither of you suffers from claustrophobia," Slocum apologized. "Two whole guests is taxing the limits of this house's hospitality."

"It's no problem," Detective Perry assured him. Sergeant Morino appeared to be distracted; he was looking under Slocum's chair as though he might find his ball there.

"Have you thought of anything else that might help us?" the detective asked as he propped a small spiral notebook on his leg.

"No. Baba was fine when I saw him last. He was on his way to another appointment."

"Is that right? I don't think you mentioned that yesterday." Perry arched his eyebrows and held them that way, creating an unconscious desire in Slocum to answer quickly and save him from a sore, overworked forehead.

"I didn't think it was unusual. That was what you asked me before."

"Baba Ahimsa only saw people on Saturday mornings," the detective told him.

"Well, that can't be right because he saw me yesterday and he said he had someone else to see too."

"Who?"

"He said it was 'another blind date.'"

"What do you think he meant by that?"

"Well he didn't know me ahead of time, so I guess he meant he didn't know who he was seeing next."

"Why do you think he agreed to see people he didn't even know on a day when he didn't ordinarily see people?" Perry asked.

"As I understand it, Lucas Dayton — I mean Marcus Beecham — called several months ago to set up my appointment."

"Which one was it, Lucas or Marcus?"

"They're the same person. He uses more than one name."

"Why?"

"I don't know."

Although he kept his pen poised over his pad, Detective Perry didn't take any notes. His eyes stayed focused on Slocum's.

Sergeant Morino seemed to be studying something that was written in the air between himself and Slocum's chest.

"What's the deal here anyway?" Slocum asked. "I thought Baba died a natural death."

Perry held up his hand. "Let's just continue on for now. I'll fill you in later. So I gather, then, that you were looking forward to your appointment with Mr. Ahimsa for quite some time?"

"No, I just found out about it an hour or two before I went up there."

Perry shook his head. "I'm confused."

"You see, Lucas — I mean Marcus — must've made the appointment and then later decided that I'd be the one to go."
"Why?"
"I don't know."
Perry shook his head again and glanced at his silent companion. "Are you getting this?" he asked.
Morino's head inched from side to side.
"Let me start at the beginning," Slocum suggested.
"Go ahead."
He retold his peculiar tale, beginning with the pig postcard and ending with his phone call to the Long Marine Lab after seeing Saddhu Ramba. He included virtually everything he could remember, which lengthened the account into a twenty-five minute monologue. Neither listener showed any sign of believing it, not believing it, being amused, amazed, or even especially interested. It occurred to Slocum that this non-responsive listening was probably a difficult skill to acquire. Perhaps there was a class on it at the police academy. When he'd finally finished, he leaned back in his wooden chair with a sense of relief. The account was as much a confession of his own idiocy as an explanation of anything. He felt purged of some indeterminate, uncomfortable feeling. Maybe these cops should moonlight as shrinks.
"Let me go over a few things," Detective Perry said.
"Sure."
"You walked with Mr. Ramba from between nine and ten this morning and then you saw him on a trail in Lighthouse Field?"
"That's right." Slocum was bewildered. "What's that got to do with anything?"
The black man held up a hand again. "Bear with me just a little longer, please. Did Mr. Ramba say or do anything unusual while you were with him?"
"Wait a minute. Did something happen to him too?"
Sergeant Morino spoke for the first time. "He's dead," he announced in a very educated, modulated voice.
"Dead?"
"A cerebral hemorrhage in the same part of the brain as Baba's," Morino told him.

"Does that suggest anything?" Perry asked.

"Suggest anything?" Slocum echoed.

"Do you think it's a coincidence?" Morino asked.

"A coincidence?"

"Tell him about the bruises," Perry said to his partner.

"Baba had a small bruise on the back of his head which was consistent with falling onto rocky ground from a standing position, assuming he had undergone a burst aneurysm. Ramba has a bruise in almost exactly the same location, and the ground was soft under him."

"Tell him about the holes," Perry prompted again.

"They both have minute needle marks just under the cranial bones behind their ears."

"So what do you think, Mr. Happler?" Detective Perry asked.

Slocum was feeling sick; his gorge rose and subsided twice before he could reply. "Somebody killed them," he managed to croak out.

"That's what we think," Perry said.

"Was it you?" Morino asked.

"No!" The idea shocked him. "That's ridiculous. I had no reason to harm them. I didn't even know either one until I met them this week. I told you all that."

"Ah yes. Your story of intrigue and all that. I must admit I've never heard anything quite like it," Perry told him. "How about you, Tom?"

Morino shook his head. "Never. I thought it was very creative, though — showed a lot of imagination."

"Look," Slocum pleaded. "It's obvious now what's been going on. I've been framed."

"By this Marcus character?" Perry asked.

"Exactly. It's all been an elaborate ruse to get me on the spot when the murders took place."

"And leave you with an unlikely story to tell?" Morino added.

"Yes! Can't you see it?"

The two policemen exchanged looks which were unreadable to Slocum but apparently meant something to them.

"Can you substantiate what you've been telling us?" Morino asked.

"What do you mean?"

"Whatever. Tell us how to contact Marcus or Lucy. Or show us some evidence that what you're saying is true."

"Well, I don't know how to find them — they were clever about that. I see that now. But I can describe the cars they drove and what they look like. And — wait a minute — I saved the postcard that started all this." He jumped up and moved toward the kitchen alcove.

Morino leapt to his feet too. "Whoa, pardner. Slow down there. I'll go with you and we'll move *real* slowly. Okay?"

"Sure." Slocum walked carefully to his junk drawer, where all the small odds and ends of his life piled up. "I know right where it is."

"Great," Morino answered noncommittally, moving next to Slocum.

"Hey, it's gone! I could've sworn I had it in here."

Slocum opened the nearest cabinet and peered in.

"Do you want some help looking?" Morino asked.

"Sure."

"So you're giving us permission to look, right?"

"That's what I said," Slocum answered impatiently. "Now where the hell is it?"

Morino moved back into the living room as Slocum kept searching.

"Could you come over here?" Detective Perry asked a few moments later.

Slocum walked over to where the two policemen were crouched near the coffee table.

Morino gestured under the chair. "Is that yours?" he asked.

Slocum got down on his knees. There was a small clear plastic packet with bits of metal in it lying on the rug. "No," he replied. "I don't think so."

Morino produced a white handkerchief and fished out the packet with it.

"I don't even sew," Slocum told them. The item seemed to be a sewing kit, or at least a packet of needles.

"These aren't sewing needles," Perry told him. "They're acupuncture needles."

Morino looked at his partner.

"My back, Tom. Remember when I was seeing Mrs. Chen?"

The sergeant nodded. "Look at this," he added.

Detective Perry and Slocum leaned over. Two of the needles were stained dark red. Slocum gasped involuntarily.

"You're under arrest, Mr. Happler," Perry told him.

Morino read him his rights as Perry handcuffed him.

Thirteen

In the unmarked police car on the way downtown, Detective Perry assured Slocum that he would check out his story.

"I have to admit," he told him, "that it's hard to imagine you'd invent a story that stupid."

"Maybe he's stupid," Sergeant Morino said in a deadpan voice from behind the wheel.

"I'm not," Slocum told him. "I'm a graduate student."

"So you're paying thousands of dollars to study something useless so you can get out of school and not have a job?"

"Well, yeah. I guess that sums it up. But they only let smart people do it."

"Uh huh."

The handcuffs hurt and the blue vinyl backseat smelled like Lysol and puke. Slocum wasn't happy.

"Of course you might be crazy. That would explain it," Perry said.

"I think he's crazy," Morino told his partner.

"I'm not crazy," Slocum protested.

"Crazy people always say that," Morino replied, making a left hand turn onto the street that led to the downtown police station.

"Are you guys always like this? Or is it just me?" Slocum asked.

Morino turned to Perry. "Paranoia," he pronounced.

Slocum gritted his teeth and gave up.

As the car approached the city hall complex, he saw that there was some kind of demonstration being held outside the police station.

"It's the homeless again," Morino announced. "I'm getting tired of this."

"Why don't you park on Church Street and we'll go in the side door," Perry suggested.

"Sure thing."

As the car slid into a parking space alongside the low brick building, Slocum noticed an elderly homeless woman lurking in some nearby bushes. She was wearing a black garbage bag as a poncho, and a small silver whistle dangled from a red lanyard around her neck. As the two policemen climbed out of the car, the woman scrabbled for her whistle, clenched it between yellowed teeth, and began to blow frantically.

"What the hell?" Morino exclaimed.

"Let's get him in there fast," Perry called, opening the back door for Slocum.

As the prisoner awkwardly propelled himself, handcuffed, out of the vehicle, a horde of protesters rounded the corner and descended on the patch of sidewalk beside the car door. There must've been thirty or forty of them, a mixture of street people, college students, and something in between — perhaps students who shopped for clothes at the dump or young upwardly mobile homeless.

The crowd radiated raw hostility towards the detectives and Slocum. As several raggedy men moved forward, Morino and Perry flanked their prisoner and the black man spoke loudly.

"This is official police business. Clear a path, please."

"Clear *this,* pig," one of the men replied, giving him the finger and a nasty grin.

"Don't let the three little pigs into their house!" a hoarse woman's voice called from the back of the crowd.

The protesters closed ranks and glared. Slocum held up his handcuffs.

"There's only two little pigs," he told the crowd.

"Free the brother!" a vaguely familiar voice shouted. Flinch stepped out from behind a bearded Neanderthal and pointed at Slocum. He was wearing jeans, a fatigue jacket, and high black boots.

"He was only sleeping in the park!" Flinch asserted.

The crowd roared and edged forward.

"That's not true!" Perry called. "This man is a suspect in a...."

"Get 'em!" Flinch interrupted, and all hell broke loose.

* * *

A minute later, policemen poured out of the building to rescue the detectives, who were buried under two discrete piles of protesters. Flinch and Slocum were around the corner, running at full speed, which wasn't very fast. Slocum was hindered by his handcuffs, while the fierce-looking homeless man was handicapped by his clunky boots and a tendency to zigzag for no apparent reason.

Slocum was following his liberator, his mind inert as he churned his legs. Later it would occur to him that if he'd thought about it, he'd never have run. The melee outside the station catalyzed an aggregation of feelings that he had been collecting since the policemen had arrived at his house. When Flinch grabbed his arm and pulled, Slocum was lost in an internal drama, starring fear, grief, anger, and confusion. His body responded instinctively to the opportunity to escape, releasing a surge of adrenaline. The next thing he knew, he was pounding down the sidewalk, heedless of the ramifications of his action.

Flinch headed for the Mission Hill railroad tunnel, and they reached the dimly lit sanctuary with no evidence of pursuit. The tunnel was old and crudely finished. Timbers shored up the roof, and there was a great deal of litter plastered up against the wooden walls.

Huddling along the side, gasping for breath, Slocum asked, "What's next?"

Flinch wheezed and bent forward at the waist, placing his grimy hands on his denim-clad knees. He smelled like dirt.

"That depends," he finally replied, the words emerging with difficulty.

"On what?"

"What they were bringing you in for and whether you did it."

"Oh. Well, actually it was murder, and no I didn't do it."

"Who did?"

"I think it was that guy you told me to stay away from."

"Tell me again."

"I think it was...."

"No, not that. I want you to look me in the eye and tell me you didn't do it."

"It's too dark in here to see your eyes."

"So guess where they are, okay? Jesus, you can really be a pain, you know that?"

"Yeah, I guess so. Alright — here goes. I did not kill anyone. I was framed."

There was a pause.

"I believe you," Flinch told him. "So here's what we're gonna do. There's a tourist train due any minute — you know, the one that runs from the Boardwalk up to that fake old town in the redwoods? So we'll hop on the back — it goes slow so it doesn't run over the pond scum that sleep in here sometimes. There's like a little porch on the back of the last car — it's a snap."

"Even with handcuffs?" Slocum held up his manacled hands.

"Oh yeah. The handcuffs. Well, we'll give it a shot, huh?"

"Have you got any other plans?" Slocum asked.

"Yeah, I'm having lunch with the fucking President but I'll just no-show the bastard."

"No, I mean for what to do to get away from the police."

"Oh. Nope."

"In that case we'll give it a shot."

"Right. The secret is getting a running start without tripping on the goddamn ties. Then you just... hold on! Here it comes." Flinch shoved Slocum up against the wall. "Don't move 'til I tell you."

"Right."

The steam locomotive was terrifyingly huge, loud, and suddenly near. The ground shook and Slocum smelled an overwhelming potpourri of wood smoke, grease, hot metal, and cinders. The train wasn't proceeding nearly as slowly as he expected, which inspired even more fear. Abruptly, his life seemed to be reduced to spending many years in prison or becoming mangled underneath an antique train. And some maniac homeless guy was in charge of which fate would prevail. He felt as though something extremely heavy was resting in the bottom of his stomach. Maybe an iron. How was he going to move when it was time?

As the three passenger cars rolled by, looking as big as houses in the shadowy light, it suddenly seemed impossible that Slocum's predicament would turn out okay. Much as he sometimes sensed the perfectness of everything, he was now sure that nothing made sense, and that by definition he and everyone else were doomed to play out their tragic roles. Strangely, he experienced a modicum of relief from arriving at this completely negative point of view. At least he didn't have to wonder any more.

"Now!" Flinch shouted in the din of the tunnel, running forward as the caboose appeared.

Slocum struck out behind him, almost losing his footing immediately. It was obvious that Flinch had done this before. The man approached the wrought iron railing and in one smooth motion pulled himself up and over onto the train proper.

Slocum ran and jumped moments later, managing to get his hands and handcuffs over the railing and one foot somewhere that felt useful. Almost immediately he began slipping back and a part of him said "See, I told you so." But another part replied "Fuck this!" and wriggled forward. Flinch grabbed Slocum's wrists and pulled. Between the two of their efforts, Slocum finally tumbled painfully onto the metal floor grating of the caboose's back porch. A rough-edged throbbing in his shoulder accompanied his pessimistic mood.

"All right!" Flinch exclaimed, hunkering down on the grating.

Slocum adjusted his position and discovered a gash on his shin and an aching bruise on his right hip.

"Way to go!" Flinch added. "You must be some kind of athlete or something. I've never seen anybody do that on their first try, even without the bracelets."

"Then why the hell did you suggest it?"

"Well I knew I could do it and I couldn't think of anything else."

"Great. Just great."

"Hey man, what are you bitching about? Here we are. Enjoy the ride, huh?"

Slocum caught his breath and sat up, acutely aware of his shoulder, hip, and shin. The train was picking up speed as it chugged through the warehouse district on the northwestern edge of town. Most of the buildings were metal Quonset huts. They looked like huge whale skeletons.

"Why are you doing this?" Slocum asked his rescuer.

Flinch shrugged. "The shrink at the vet's hospital said I have poor impulse control. I guess I just like stirring things up now and then." His grin was surrounded by patchy stubble; the burn scars on his chin and cheek formed islands of hairlessness. Slocum noticed that one of them was shaped just like Australia, but he decided not to point that out. Flinch's eyes were scary. Slocum wasn't sure why, but he found it difficult to look at them for more than a second or two.

"I'm Slocum Happler," he told the man.

"It sucks."

"What?"

"Your name — it sucks. Let's see... I think we'll call you 'Sloke'."

"We?"

"No. Let's go for 'Hap.' How's that sound?"

"Whatever." As the train roared on into the forest, the dank air grew cooler. "So who's this 'we?'" Slocum drew his knees up to his chest and crossed his arms, rubbing his sore shoulder. He felt like dog doo-doo.

"You'll see."

"You've got another plan, don't you?"

Flinch nodded.

"Do we have to swim a few miles or fly this time?"

Flinch shook his head, his greasy brown hair falling across his forehead. "You're kind of a jerk, aren't you?" he said.

"No."

That was the only conversation for the next few miles.

Fourteen

"It's gonna be time to jump soon. Just do it the way I do it," Flinch said.

"Wait a minute. I don't want to jump. I hurt all over from getting on," Slocum protested. "Why can't we wait until the train stops and then climb off?"

"The conductors hang out back here once they get everybody's tickets."

"Oh." Slocum thought a moment. "Maybe we could get on the roof."

"That's stupid. Anyway it's time to jump."

"Hold it! I think we should...."

Flinch vaulted over the railing, momentarily landing on his feet beside the track, and then rolling into the underbrush. Slocum short-circuited his brain by immediately launching his injured body after him. In mid-air he fully realized what he'd done and braced himself for the impending impact. As a result, his landing was stiff and awkward. He fell heavily, somersaulting out of control into a bush with nasty spiked leaves. If Flinch's landing was reminiscent of Aikido, Slocum's suggested pro wrestling.

He was afraid to move and find out what new injuries he'd sustained. Most everything hurt at this point, but what would he do if he'd broken his arm, or worse? Maybe if he just lived in this bush from now on, everything would work out okay. Slocum closed his eyes and tried to settle into his new home. He seemed to be mostly upside down. One foot was hooked on something and the other one, unshod, pressed against his sore butt.

He heard someone coming and tried to ignore him.

"Didn't anyone ever teach you how to fall?" Flinch asked the bush.

Slocum opened his eyes and glared at the homeless man's knees. "No. Why should they?"

"I dunno. I learned in the army." Flinch moved forward and grabbed a couple of branches. "Come on. We've got to get moving."

Slocum groaned and began to untangle himself. It hurt a lot.

"Anything broke?"

"I don't think so. Have you seen my shoe?"

"Yeah. Here."

"Thanks." Slocum sat next to the bush and bled into his shoe as he tried to slip it on. The handcuffs didn't help matters.

"You're a mess," Flinch told him.

"No kidding."

"We've got band-aids."

"There's that 'we' again." Slocum finished putting on his shoe and slowly drew himself erect. He seemed to have added a sprained ankle, a gash over one of his eyebrows, cuff-shaped gouges on both wrists, and about a million deep scratches and bruises.

"Follow me and keep quiet," Flinch counseled. He moved across the tracks and squeezed between two large ferns.

Slocum limped along behind him. In just a few moments the two men were moving through the redwood forest itself.

It was dark and cool. Almost everything was either green or reddish brown. Occasionally the sun penetrated the high canopy and spotlit a tableau of rocks, ferns, and whatever debris the trees had deposited beneath themselves. There was something magical about these golden scenes, although as Slocum moved through them he did tend to bleed on them.

Most of the sounds in the forest filtered down from above. Jays chattered, squirrels clattered on long claws to the hidden side of tree trunks, and the redwoods themselves creaked audibly as breezes shifted them.

Flinch moved like a proverbial Indian, adding little or no sound to the environment. In his heavy black boots, this was no small feat. Slocum's limp grew more pronounced as he hiked, increasing his self-consciousness about the racket he was creating. Eventually the birds began calling from up ahead of the two men, warning the woods of their approach.

The air was rich and moist, redolent with the pine-like odor of the big trees. An occasional bay tree lent a tang to the mixture of smells, while the earth added periodic doses of decomposition and decay.

It was like travelling to another planet or an alternate universe where all the norms were different. Certainly the dimensions bore no similarity to anywhere else Slocum had ever been. The trees towered hundreds of feet above him, and some were probably twenty feet in circumference. Exposed tree roots were like monstrous snakes living simultaneously above and below the earth.

There was very little underbrush, which was handy since Flinch didn't appear to be following a trail. He did seem to know exactly where he was going, though. Without hesitation he led Slocum further and further into the forest. Although the train ride had disoriented him, Slocum figured that they must be in some remote part of Henry Cowell State Park. He was hoping to get a chance to sit down and think through things soon. Maybe they'd arrive at a campsite in the next few minutes. His ankle was especially interested in becoming stationary, it might just decide to dictate terms to the rest of him.

Flinch stopped and hooted twice. Three hoots were returned from just ahead, then Flinch hooted once more.

"Okay," the homeless man said. "Stick close to me and let me handle things."

"What things?" Slocum asked. "What is there to handle?"

But Flinch was already moving again and Slocum had to get limping along after him. It was another fifty yards through a particularly magnificent circle of trees before the twosome encountered the other hooter, and all the rest.

It was an encampment with half a dozen tents, several crude lean-tos, and two large campfire pits, one of which was blazing away. Four men and two dogs sat or reclined by the fire. They were all filthy. When Slocum entered the clearing behind Flinch, two men and one of the dogs rose. The fire flickered yellow and orange light on them. One man was huge, maybe six foot six and three hundred pounds. He had an unlined moon face. The other one had the look of an ancient Country and Western singer. He was lean and his face was leathery and wrinkled. A straw cowboy hat perched low on his forehead, completing the image.

The dog was a young version of the generic third-world stray — tan, short haired, big eared, pointy nosed, medium sized, and very thin. He trotted over to Slocum, sniffed his bloody shoe, and wagged his tail uncertainly. Slocum reached down with both his cuffed hands and scratched him behind the ear. His bony tail whipped from side to side like a berserk metronome.

"Tirebiter likes him," one of the seated men pointed out in a low, gruff voice. Like the others, he was in his mid-to-late forties. A long flowing beard and wildly tangled long black hair gave him a biker look.

"That doesn't mean shit," the enormous man replied in a surprisingly high voice, glaring at Slocum, who plopped down on the ground and continued to pet the dog. "Tirebiter doesn't know anything."

"Who the fuck is he? And what's he doing here?" the cowboy asked in a classic West Texas accent. His voice was ruined from smoking. His eyes never changed expression despite the force of his words.

Flinch held up a hand. "Calm down, huh? You know I wouldn't bring an asshole up here. Well, actually he is kind of an asshole, but the cops are after him for murder and I think he's gettin' a raw deal."

"Does it talk?" the fourth man asked. He was clean shaven and his voice was smoother than the others. He wore a blue down vest over a red flannel shirt. Instead of boots, he sported high-top white tennis shoes.

"I talk," Slocum told him.

"Why's he bleeding?" the big man asked Flinch.

Flinch grinned evilly and hunkered down next to the fire. "The train," he answered.

Everyone smiled, even the other dog, which was damned peculiar.

"Train — one; asshole — zero," the biker guy proclaimed with a throaty chuckle.

"No, no," Flinch corrected. "He did it, even with the cuffs."

"But it hurt a lot," Slocum announced.

"Hey, are you from Texas?" the cowboy asked.

Slocum nodded, which hurt. "Austin. You sound like you're from Lubbock."

"Odessa. Good guess, though."

"Well, before he bleeds to death, we better settle this," the big man said.

"Settle it?" Slocum echoed. This didn't sound too promising. He pictured hand-to-hand combat with the giant guy.

"Sounds good," Flinch agreed.

"I thought you were on *my* side," Slocum complained.

"I am. Just stand up."

"I don't want to."

"Do it anyway," the big man told him.

He stood up. Tirebiter the dog wandered off.

The man snapped his fingers and the other dog got up and moved towards Slocum. It was an old, very large, bushy dog. Slocum wasn't scared of it, although he had no idea what was going to happen next. The dog was mostly black and gray, except for white boots on her hind legs and an age-whitened muzzle. Beautiful brown eyes gazed serenely at Slocum as she approached. Somehow, when the dog got closer, Slocum could sense that she was a she. It was obvious that he had no reason to worry about a creature as sweet as this.

"What's the deal?" the large man asked the dog.

She slowly circled Slocum and then sniffed his hand. Her furry tail swayed back and forth a couple of times, and then she returned to her place by the fire.

"Whoa!" the clean-shaven man exclaimed.

"Did you see that?" the cowboy added.

The big man strode up to Slocum and held out his hand. "Call me Buddha Boy," he told him.

Slocum placed both his hands in Buddha Boy's giant one, feeling like an eight year old.

"I'm Slo... I mean, uh... hey, Flinch, what's that nickname you gave me?"

"I've got a new one. Twice. We're gonna call you Twice."

The other men nodded their heads as if this made sense.

The cowboy spoke next. "Verlin," he said. "I'm Verlin."

"Terhune," the biker announced.

"Gidget," the clean-shaven man told Slocum.

"Gidget?"

"It's a long story."

Slocum and the others sidled up to the fire and sprawled beside it.

"I'll get the medicine kit," Flinch told Slocum as he walked off.

"So will somebody explain to me about the dog? What was that all about?" Slocum asked.

Buddha Boy spoke. "Her name's Karma. I didn't name her. She had that on a tag when I found her years ago. She can tell who's okay and who isn't — by the way they smell, I guess. If she thinks someone's okay, she wags her tail once. If she doesn't like you, she just walks off. And she's almost always right."

"I find that hard to believe."

"It's fucking weird," Verlin agreed. "But it's true."

Flinch showed up with the "first aid kit," which turned out to be a paper bag with a box of band-aids and several tongue depressors in it. As he handed it to Slocum he examined the cut on his brow.

"Needs stitches, man."

"Gonna get a band-aid," Terhune replied.

Slocum began placing band-aids on his largest cuts and scratches. Tirebiter settled in next to him. Something was nagging though. "The dog wagged twice, right? I thought you said she wags once or not at all."

"Hey, you just figured out your fucking nickname," Buddha Boy told him.

"She never wagged twice before," Gidget said.

"I think Karma really likes you," Flinch added.

"You guys aren't bullshitting?" Slocum asked.

"Listen up," Buddha Boy replied. "When I first got her, I didn't pay much attention to all this. I had a career and everything and I just wasn't open to weird shit."

"What was your career?"

The giant looked uncomfortable. He watched the fire as he answered sheepishly. "I was a lawyer. But then the P.T.S.D. kicked in and I was out of there."

"P.T.S.D.?"

"Post-Traumatic Stress Disorder." He gestured at the others with a huge thumb. "We were all in 'Nam."

"Together?"

"Naw," Terhune answered. "Although I saw Buddha Boy over there in a bar once."

"You can remember something like that?"

"Believe me, it was memorable. He was kicking the shit out of three sailors."

The big man was embarrassed again. "I used to have a drinking problem," he explained. "Anyway, I would meet people and be friends or whatever and then later it would turn out that whatever Karma thought about them would be right. I've had her twelve years and I swear she's hardly ever liked someone that turned out to be a snake or the other way around either. Sometimes it really blows my mind."

"Remember that last guy?" Verlin drawled.

"That was radical," Terhune added.

Buddha Boy explained. "She caught this dude trying to rip-off my jacket and tore him up pretty bad."

"This dog here? Karma?"

"It's like she's got an on-off switch somewhere and some people set it off," Buddha Boy told Slocum.

"Yeah," Flinch agreed. "Karma can be your best friend or one hell of a bitch."

Whether he was still talking about the dog or not wasn't clear to Slocum. He finally decided that Flinch didn't exactly fit the profile of an inveterate punster.

"Hmm. So you guys are survivalists or something?"

"Whatta'ya mean?" Flinch asked aggressively.

"I just mean you live here in the woods, right?"

"Well, duh, Sherlock. Next you're gonna ask why we named the mutt 'Tirebiter,'" Flinch replied.

"Does he bite tires?"

"Yup."

"Why?"

"Why? How the fuck do I know why?" Flinch seemed offended by the question. "Why don't you ask him?"

Verlin laughed. It was a dry, rattling sound.

"Tell us about the murder," Gidget suggested. "Did the guy deserve it?"

"No. There were two guys," Slocum explained. "Holy men, really. I'm being framed by this other guy that's real ambitious, I guess." He stared into the fire and the dancing flames soothed him.

"Ambitious?" Verlin asked.

"Spiritually ambitious. I don't know. He may have other reasons."

"So you're up shit creek?" Buddha Boy asked.

"You got it. They found the murder weapons at my place and I was the last guy to see the victims." He placed a band-aid on the back of his hand and winced.

"Second to last," Buddha Boy corrected, holding up two massive fingers.

"Yeah, right. Second to last."

"If you've got all that bleeding stopped, we've got some clothes and a sleeping bag you can use," Terhune told Slocum. His voice was casual and friendly.

"Whose?" Flinch asked, his tone fierce again.

"Now don't get upset, Flinch," Terhune the biker began, "but they picked up Junior on a seventy-two hour hold again."

"Aw shit, Terhune. Fuck you. I thought you were gonna watch him."

Terhune shrugged, but Slocum could sense that he was scared of the smaller man.

After a pause, Flinch released another explosive stream of curses. His fists were clenching and unclenching rhythmically.

"Let's be nice," Buddha Boy said.

"Fuck you too," Flinch replied.

"Hey, we've got company, man," Gidget interjected. "You know how Junior is."

"Is this the Junior I know?" Slocum asked Flinch.

"Yeah. He's got a few problems so the cops grab him for psychiatric observation sometimes. Shit!"

Tirebiter's head lifted up, he surveyed the situation, and then decided to go back to sleep. Karma seemed to be watching Slocum with one eye open and one eye closed.

"Who's cooking dinner tonight?" Verlin asked.

"You are, you moron," Flinch answered.

"Why don't you take a walk?" Buddha Boy suggested, his tone steely.

The two men locked eyes for several seconds. Flinch tensed as if to launch himself, but then relaxed slightly, pushed himself up, and swaggered off.

"Welcome to Camp Friendly," Gidget told Slocum.

Fifteen

The evening passed. Dinner was a can of chili, two pieces of white bread, and as many over-ripe bananas as you cared to eat. Two more men showed up during the meal. How they found the place in the dark was hard for Slocum to imagine.

Pope was an obvious alcoholic who didn't say much. He was even skinnier than Verlin and didn't seem long for this world. Just moving around was a complex challenge for his eroding motor skills. He smelled like a sewer.

Guppy was Slocum's age, far too young to have been in Vietnam. He said he was Pope's apprentice in a proud, reedy voice. He was probably the saddest one, from Slocum's perspective. The others had become homeless through a process of attrition, forced on them as a side effect of their war experiences. Chubby Guppy was drawn to the outlaw lifestyle by a self-produced interior fantasy that transmuted conditions such as being dirty into "a dose of reality" and cheap food into "living off the land." He smelled like a wet dog.

Supposedly, Pope knew a guy who could pick the locks on the handcuffs. Early in the morning, Guppy would go find the guy and bring him back.

Later, as Slocum lay in Junior's mildewed red sleeping bag, the prospect of losing his cuffs became a pre-eminent concern. It was impossible to settle on a sleeping position that didn't torture his lacerated wrists. His shoulder, hip, and ankle hurt like hell too, throbbing with each beat of his heart. He was going to have to be a lot more tired before he could fall asleep.

All in all, Slocum felt as though he'd reached a new nadir in his life. He was thoroughly miserable on every level.

Intellectually, he was only too aware of a few basic facts. He was wanted for murder, lost in the woods with a gang of burnt-out vets, and was probably too beat up to even walk any more.

Emotionally, he was scared, angry, hurting, and sad. Instead of politely taking turns, the feelings inundated him en masse, sloshing around inside like a spoiled stew.

Physically, aside from his injuries, Slocum was cold, the beans in his gut were generating gas, and the stink of mold, stale liquor, and sweat assaulted his nostrils. Junior's sleeping bag was the most odorific inanimate object Slocum had ever been forced to experience.

On a spiritual level, Slocum was merely very confused, but somehow this was the worst. It was as if he'd had his psychic foundation pulled out from under him — a foundation he hadn't consciously known about until it was no longer in place. If he had the benefit of a firm place to stand, all the rest would be so much easier to bear.

Eventually he fell asleep. At some point during the night, he awoke to find both dogs huddled against him, one on either side. As if on cue, Karma farted; it was an epic production, which woke her up. Her eyes slowly focused on Slocum's and there was a loving kindness in them that was so simple and clear that Slocum began to cry. Tirebiter woke up and licked the tears from his cheeks as Karma watched with her Mother Theresa eyes. The air smelled like farts and Slocum cried and cried like a baby.

*   *   *

In the morning, by the time Slocum struggled to his feet, visited the crude latrine, and outfitted himself in Junior's filthy, voluminous clothes, the guy that could pick locks had already arrived. He fit right in. His name was Lee and he was practically a zombie. Even breathing entailed a major effort for Lee, let alone talking or moving. He just didn't have any energy at all.

He was probably around thirty years old but it was hard to look at anything besides his huge spud nose. It was crimson red and the pores were grotesquely enlarged, creating a distinct grid that exaggerated the nasal topography to the eye.

Slocum sat next to Flinch on a log in the sunlight and tried not to stare at Lee's nose as he fiddled with the bloodstained handcuffs.

It was a gorgeous morning. A few seconds of not looking at Lee's nose was sufficient to establish that. Despite his physical discomfort and hunger, Slocum couldn't help but appreciate the morning light in the woods around him.

The towering trees cast long shadows across the brown, patterned forest floor. Looking closer, Slocum saw that the patterns were formed by the accumulation of thousands of sprigs of redwood needles. The needles prevented any delineation between light and dark from becoming too stark, softening the edges with their feathery outline. Partially shadowed stumps, logs, and ferns added to the impressionistic mood, creating complex, impossible shapes as they distorted the lines of the trees' projections.

When Slocum cut down his field of vision to just a few square inches, there still seemed to be an infinite amount of detail available for perusal. Crawling amongst the tangled mat of redwood needles were a variety of insects, ranging from little black dots with legs to inch-long purple-backed beetles. The insects' patterns of movement as they fulfilled their daily tasks created another superimposed level of dark and light. Slocum felt that if he could keep looking closer and deeper, he'd discover an endless series of fresh tableaux to study.

"No more fires while you're here," Flinch told him, interrupting the process. He spoke in a tone of voice that implied they were in the middle of a conversation. Slocum wondered if he'd missed anything. "It's too risky," Flinch explained. "And check this out. Guppy brought back the newspaper. You made page one, buddy."

He held up the front page and Slocum reached for it, forgetting his cuffs.

"Hey," Lee mumbled.

"Sorry."

Flinch positioned the paper so that Slocum could survey it by turning his head. His passport photo stared back at him from the center of the page. It could've been a composite depiction of the quintessential terrorist. His eyes were half closed and his mouth had been captured between smiles. The dark stubble on his cheeks was reminiscent of Yassar Arafat.

"I look like a killer," he lamented.

Lee glanced up from his work and studied him, a bobby pin gripped between his teeth. "Amen, brother," he intoned.

"It says you're studying consciousness," Flinch told Slocum. "What the fuck does that mean?"

"It's philosophy and political theory — stuff like that. You know — Karl Marx, the existentialists — that sort of thing."

"Who the fuck cares about that? What's it got to do with anything?"

"Right now, not much."

"Damn straight."

The article also stated that the "murder suspect" might be "associated with a cult" or be "dangerously disturbed." Detective Perry was quoted as saying "we're still in the preliminary stages of our investigation, but the suspect's escape doesn't encourage our views on his innocence."

Seven people were arrested at the mini-riot outside the police station, but none of them were believed to be connected with Slocum. Sergeant Morino sustained "multiple contusions" and was "nursing a sprained knee." Nonetheless, he was "mobilizing an old-fashioned posse" to "track down the wanted man."

Slocum was described as a "Texas import" and a "recent newcomer to the Santa Cruz community." An elderly neighbor said that he seemed "as nice as can be" and "was always a gentleman."

Two separate front page articles served as lengthy obituaries for the dead men. The mayor, a lesbian health food store owner, stated that "the community and the entire world have lost vital resources in our struggle to become one with compassion." Photographs of Baba and Saddhu were so evocative of Slocum's experiences of them that he discovered tears welling up in his eyes. He realized that he'd had very little chance to grieve in any normal way.

"Got something in your eye?" Flinch asked.

"You're a real sensitive New Age guy, aren't you?"

"What? What'd I say?"

"I'm crying, you asshole."

"Hey, okay. Great. Go to it."

"Thanks a lot."

"Got it," Lee announced, clicking open one of the cuffs.

"Thank God," Slocum said, moving his free hand up to wipe away a tear.

Buddha Boy strolled over. "They're gonna be searching the woods, I bet." His bulk blocked the sun, which created a spectacular corona around his silhouette.

"Aw, they'll never find us," Flinch replied. "That park dickhead has been trying for months."

"He doesn't use dogs or dozens of volunteer deputies, does he?"

"Fuck no, man. They wouldn't put that clown in charge of anything."

"Should I be taking off?" Slocum asked. "Is that what you mean?"

"No. I just think we should plan what we'll do if they show up," Buddha Boy replied.

"Well I can't hang around here forever anyway," Slocum told him. "I need to clear my name and I'm not going to do it up here."

"You're too hot," Flinch told him. "We're not talking about a traffic ticket. This is fucking murder. Anybody sees you on the street, they're gonna call the cops."

"I've got a friend who can help," Slocum told him. "He can do the legwork to start with."

"That sounds good," Buddha Boy commented.

Lee unlocked the remaining handcuff. "Can I keep these?" he asked.

"Be my guest," Slocum answered. "I hope I never see those damn things again."

"Thanks, man." Lee wandered off, clutching the cuffs as if they were a newly opened Christmas present.

Slocum stood and waved his arms around, which made his shoulder hurt like hell. His ankle wasn't happy either. But at least he wasn't bleeding any more.

"How do you feel?" Buddha Boy asked.

"Like shit. Most everything hurts."

"That's rough."

"Rougher than a cob," Verlin added as he joined the threesome. "And there's something you ought to know, Twice.

If they offer a reward? I'll turn you in." The old cowboy was grinning apologetically.

"Me too," Flinch added. "Nothing personal."

Slocum thought about it. "I don't blame you. This isn't exactly a lavish lifestyle you guys have got going."

"Hey, we're not here because we're poor," Buddha Boy told him, his round face mobilizing a frown. "We want to live here. It's a privilege to live here. Understand?"

"Sure. Sorry."

"Let's eat breakfast," Verlin suggested.

"Now you're talking," Flinch agreed. "We can make plans later."

Sixteen

After the post-meal planning session, in which it was decided that Flinch would go fetch Greg and everyone would split up and run like hell if the cops found the campsite, Slocum lay on his back on a thin foam pad and listened to stories about homeless life. From his supine perspective near the center of the clearing, the treetops formed a lacy filter, moderating the influence of the sky on the forest. As the wind nudged the higher branches, the interplay of elements constantly shifted. Slocum discovered that by squinting he could create a pleasant kaleidoscope effect.

The stories were almost always self-aggrandizing, although to Slocum's ears the vets displayed their obnoxiousness a lot more than their heroism. Apparently a certain kind of macho self-absorption was desirable in their subculture.

"We're the elite of the homeless," Gidget told him at one point. "We've got survival skills, no-shit attitudes, and we can back up our attitudes just as far as anybody wants to take it."

"Every man here has killed," Verlin added in his West Texas twang, "At least once. Pope was a sniper in 'Nam — he's chalked up hundreds. Right, Pope?"

The alcoholic grunted his assent. He probably couldn't even hold silverware, let alone a gun. Slocum found the whole experience terribly sad, so he concentrated on the redwood kaleidoscope and his own thoughts about his predicament.

He needed to provide the police a more likely suspect than himself. That was clear. But who could possibly be more likely than a guy who was on the scene both times and had apparently sequestered the murder weapons under his chair? Lucas? Not without a shitload of proof. And what would that consist of? Lucy's testimony? Yeah, right. Discovering a motive? That made sense. Why did Lucas want these men dead? Just calling it ambition didn't really answer the question. If Lucas was the beneficiary of big life insurance policies or something like that, then Slocum was in business.

He tried to think of everything he knew for sure about Lucas. His only unimpeachable sources had been the two victims. Apparently, Lucas' name was Marcus Beecham and he had been a follower of Brahmachari's over in India, along with Baba, Saddhu, and an indeterminate number of others. That was all he could remember that seemed even vaguely relevant.

Perhaps the key to Lucas' motive lay in the past. A perusal of Brahmachari's books, assuming he wrote any, might be a good place to start.

When Greg arrived later, he agreed. Following a painful hug, and a few comments on the campsite — "It's just like in the boy scouts, only different" and "Hi gang. Let's put on a show!" — Greg proposed a trip to 'Passages,' one of the spiritually oriented bookstores in town.

"Is that the one run by the Cruz Mountain people?" Slocum asked from his perch next to the campfire.

"Yeah. They should have something, don't you think?" Greg sprawled next to him and picked up a twig to fiddle with.

"Absolutely. But are you sure you want to do this? You'll be an accessory, you know."

"I've always wanted to be an accessory," Greg replied.

"Like a hat," Flinch added from his seat next to Greg.

"Or a tie," Buddha Boy said.

"I wanna be a scarf," Verlin chimed in from across the fire.

"Come on, guys. This is serious," Slocum admonished, shaking a finger at them like an annoyed parent.

"Hey, pal," Greg replied. "Don't let a few serial murders ruin your whole day."

"I like this dude," Flinch commented, reaching over and slapping Greg on the back.

"Let's see what Karma thinks," Buddha Boy said. He called over the old bushy dog, who sniffed Greg and wagged her tail once.

"She wagged twice for me," Slocum told his friend.

"Well gee-whiz, isn't that special?"

"How'd you get here?" Slocum asked.

"We hitched," Flinch answered. "I figured he'd have a car but all he had was a bike."

"Knock, knock!" a woman's voice called from the other side of the clearing. Everyone scrabbled to their feet and Tirebiter growled.

It was Lucy.

"What the hell are you doing here?" Slocum called to her as she strode forward.

Her golden hair and a crystal pendant glinted in the sunlight; she looked as lovely as ever.

"I want to help. Believe me, I had no idea what was really going on," Lucy protested. She joined the ragged group of men and dogs. "God, you're a mess," she added, surveying Slocum.

"How'd you find this place?" Flinch asked in a nasty tone of voice. Turning to Buddha Boy before she could answer, he barked out "And where the hell is Guppy? He's supposed to be the lookout this afternoon, right?"

Buddha Boy shrugged.

Lucy responded to the first question. "I followed Greg. I've been hanging around his apartment hoping he'd lead me to Slocum. I feel just terrible about what's happened."

"You were Nancy in my dream class, weren't you?" Greg accused.

Lucy nodded and hung her head. "I wouldn't trust me either if I was you guys, but give me a chance to explain. It's not the way it looks."

Suddenly Guppy sprinted into the clearing. "Cops! They're everywhere!" he gasped. "Coming up from the west trail! Dozens of them!"

"Fuckin' A," Flinch and Verlin exclaimed in unison. At any other time, it would've been funny.

"Remember the plan!" Buddha Boy called as he ran to his tent and grabbed his sleeping bag and a backpack. A moment later, he'd disappeared into the forest, Tirebiter on his heels.

"What's the plan?" Greg asked Slocum.

"Split up and run like hell."

"That's not a very good plan," Lucy commented.

As they spoke, everyone else grabbed a few belongings and took off.

"Especially when I've got a sprained ankle," Slocum reported.

"Oops," Greg replied.

"Follow me!" Lucy called, setting out purposefully in the direction she'd arrived from. "I've got my car up on Highway Nine." Seeing that neither Greg nor Slocum were moving, she turned back for a moment. "It's your only chance, you idiots!"

Slocum looked at Greg; Greg looked at Slocum. Neither one gained a whole lot from the experience.

Just then, Karma the dog, who had been an inert lump throughout the crisis, hopped up and jogged after Lucy.

"What the hell," Slocum decreed, limping badly as he began to follow too. Greg hustled over and hoisted his friend's left arm over his shoulder. As a unit they stumbled at first, but then developed a reasonable rhythm.

They never did see any policemen, although they heard them a few times. Whenever they did, they stopped and crouched, as if crouching was some totem that would protect them. A very painful forty minutes later, Slocum stood on the dirt shoulder of the two-lane highway as Lucy unlocked her small white car. Karma piled in first, without waiting for an invitation.

"Whose dog is that?" Lucy asked.

"I don't know. I thought she belonged to that really big homeless man, but here she is," Slocum answered.

"I think she's adopted us," Greg said. "Let's just get out of here and deal with it later."

"Right," Slocum agreed. He climbed in the back with the old dog, who immediately panted slobber all over his leg.

Lucy drove north on Nine, and they encountered the first few stores in Felton just three or four curves later. Felton was one of the smaller communities that ringed Santa Cruz. The rural mountain town was comprised of a six-block-long western-style downtown, surrounded by all kinds of funky neighborhoods, which were nestled in the relatively dramatic topography.

Lucy zoomed through Felton and turned right at the only traffic light in town, heading towards Scotts Valley, a bedroom community of upscale Silicon Valley commuters.

"Maybe we should figure out where we're going," Slocum suggested, discontinuing stroking the dog.

"My place," Lucy replied.

"Oh, and why is that?"

"It's private. It's safe. Have you got any better ideas?" She braked smoothly at a red light by a Taco Bell in Scotts Valley.

"It may be safe from the cops, but doesn't Lucas know where you live?" Slocum asked.

"Well, sure."

"The cops will just arrest me. Lucas is a murderer, Lucy."

"No, he isn't. That's what we need to talk about." She abruptly accelerated away from the light as if to illustrate her impatience.

"I suppose your neighbors won't notice that Public Enemy Number One happens to be staying with you?" Karma pushed her snout under his hand and he resumed petting her.

"I don't have neighbors. That's why it's ideal," Lucy replied, speeding up to pass a lumber truck. "You know where the Mystery Spot is?"

"Off of Branciforte?"

"Right. There's a dirt road back behind it and I'm staying in a cabin near the end of the road, behind a private gate."

Slocum thought it over. The Mystery Spot was an old-fashioned tourist attraction in the redwoods where gravity and magnetism were supposed to be all screwed up. Balls rolled uphill, carpenters' levels gave bizarre readings, and some people could sense 'energy' there in some mysterious fashion. Slocum had always assumed that the spot was some kind of optical illusion. Apparently it had been very popular in the fifties and early sixties. Now, it was mostly visited by busloads of Japanese tourists. It was such a big deal in Japan that it was even advertised on Tokyo television. More importantly, it was in a remote part of the countryside, about five miles east of town.

"What do you think, Greg?" Slocum finally asked.

"I can't think of anywhere else, but we'll need to keep a real good eye on little Miss Lying Bitch here."

"Right."

"Hey!" Lucy protested.

"Shut up," Slocum told her.

"Don't tell *me* to shut up."

"I already did."

"Well, don't do it again."

"Shut up," Slocum replied. This time she did.

Seventeen

The dirt road beyond the Mystery spot was probably the worst-kept thoroughfare Slocum had ever seen. Lucy averaged about five miles an hour as she negotiated its deep holes, rocks, and gullies. But her cabin turned out to be very private and even slightly attractive in a rustic, who-needs-modern-conveniences kind of way. In Slocum's experience, this type of charm lasted for about two hours, or until he had to go to the bathroom, whichever came first.

The house was basically a simple wooden box with a front porch. The exterior walls were dark blue and the trim was painted white. The forest was cleared around the building, creating a moat of weeds and dirt. A flower bed along the sunny left side of the house somewhat ameliorated this effect. Something yellow with big leaves was currently blooming. Slocum liked it, even if he couldn't identify it.

Further up the dirt road, the lane dwindled to a path and wound its way uphill through numerous young redwoods. This view implied that the small house really was on the fringe of civilization.

Karma liked it. Upon departing from the car, her tail revved up and she toddled up to the front porch, where she sprawled contentedly. Lucy stopped to pat her head on the way in and Slocum observed the dog's response — one enthusiastic wag.

"Karma says she's okay," Slocum told Greg. "I'm surprised."

"You mean that dog is actually some sort of personality barometer?"

Slocum shrugged. "According to Buddha Boy."

"Buddha Boy?"

They were standing on the porch now, Lucy having preceded them into the cabin.

"The big guy? Face like a jack-o-lantern?"

"Oh, him. He seemed like the most together one."

"Anyway, the dog's got to know something. She wagged twice for me. That's my homeless nickname, you know, Twice."

"They were a colorful bunch, weren't they?" Greg stroked his unruly beard.

"Yeah. I hope none of them got arrested," Slocum replied. "I never even got a chance to thank them — all I did was complain."

"Hey, if *we* got away, they *must've*. Flinch was telling me about all their survival skills."

"Good old Flinch." Already the entire experience in the forest was fading. Slocum's life was so out of control, so wildly accelerated at this point that even a few hours ago seemed as if it were a previous incarnation.

"So are you guys coming in or not?" Lucy asked, standing in the doorway.

"Sure, sure."

The interior of the building resembled the exterior. The walls were planks of wood, as was the floor. There was electricity and plumbing, but both were antiquated systems, displaying wires and pipes respectively on the walls. The furniture was all constructed of white PVC plastic pipe — the kind used for inexpensive patio furniture. It was basically one large room, with a curtained alcove for a bathroom. There weren't enough windows, so it was fairly dark. The house smelled like pizza, which didn't make any sense to Slocum.

"Hmm," said Greg, surveying the place from just inside the door. "One bed, huh? Well, I'm sure we'll all fit somehow. We'll just have to become real friendly, I guess."

"Guess again," Lucy told him.

"Hey," he responded. "If you figured out that you could find Slocum through me, the police will too. I can't go home."

"That's true," she conceded. "But forget about the real friendly part." She glared at him, her green eyes narrowed.

"Lighten up. I was just joking."

"Oh."

Slocum sat at the round white plastic kitchen table. The others joined him.

"You've got a hell of a lot of explaining to do," Slocum told Lucy. "What's your real name, for starters?"

"Vanessa. Vanessa Woods."

"Got any I.D.?" Greg asked.

She nodded and produced a California drivers license in that name from a pants pocket. In the picture, she had red hair and glasses. Her age was listed as twenty-six.

"Anyone want beer?" she asked as the others inspected her license.

"Absolutely," Greg replied.

"Uh huh," Slocum agreed.

Lucy/Vanessa fetched bottles of Anchor Steam and reseated herself. "I'm going to explain everything I can and then you can ask me questions," she began. "Is that okay?"

"Sure," Slocum answered. "Go to it." He hoisted his bottle of beer and gulped the cool liquid.

Lucy took a dainty sip of her beer and leaned back. She certainly was beautiful. Slocum had always been a sucker for freckles.

"Basically, someone used me just like they used you, Slocum."

"Yeah. Lucas."

"Wait. Let me tell it. You don't know everything about this."

Slocum nodded. "I'll restrain myself."

"I was a drama student at UCLA — the graduate school," Lucy said. "I am a very good actor."

"Actress," Greg corrected.

"Actor," Lucy asserted. "I was also a Zen student at the time. So it made sense that when Lucas went to hire someone, he ended up with me. This was last August. I guess I was naive or greedy or I just didn't care, but the way he explained it, it sounded okay. And it was a *lot* of money. A few weeks' work would set me up to really make a go of it down in Hollywood. I don't think he'd picked you out yet, Slocum. He just knew he'd find someone, maybe through the HistCon department. The way he eventually presented it to me was that he worked for your father — he showed me a photo of you and your dad later. He had a lot of paperwork that backed all this up too."

Lucy paused and sipped her beer again.

"But in the beginning, I guess he just avoided using specific names because he didn't have any. So like I say, he was supposed to be working for your dad, who was this rich guy who was worried about you."

"My dad drives a fork-lift," Slocum told her.

"Well anyway, we were going to embark on this big mission to raise your self-esteem and get you counseling without your knowing about it. You know how Lucas is. This all sounds so ridiculous now, but the way he did it really worked on me. He said he was an actor too — he even had me watch a video he was in."

"How'd he manage that?" Greg asked.

"I have no idea, but he was good in it. Really good." Lucy paused before continuing. "Now here's where it gets more complicated. One of the reasons I bought the father thing was that Lucas really was taking orders from someone else. He'd call this number and he'd get instructions — I listened in a few times and this man really did tell us stuff to do."

"Did he have a Texas accent?" Slocum asked.

"No, but he did have an accent of some kind. Lucas said he was your father's personal secretary."

"What kind of accent was it?" Greg asked.

"I don't know. It was like if a Frenchman learned English in England and then came over here. He'd have two accents, one superimposed over the other."

"So this guy might have been French?"

"No, no. That was just an example. I didn't recognize exactly where he was from — that's what I'm saying. It's just that I could tell it was a complicated accent — maybe Asian."

"Hmm." Slocum finished his beer and squelched a burp. "Do you know Lucas' real name?"

"No."

"I do. How about what the victims and Lucas all had in common?"

"I haven't a clue," Lucy responded. "Aren't you going to tell me?"

"We're not sharing information here. You're explaining and we're asking questions — remember?"

She nodded and made a face.

"Where does Lucas live?" Greg asked.

"I don't know where he is now, but he was staying at the Holiday Inn downtown."

"Why don't you think he did the murders?" Slocum asked. "Maybe he was hired to do them and frame somebody else."

Lucy shook her head. "No. He was on the phone to me when Saddhu Ramba was killed. He called from his motel room and I could hear the TV on in the background. This morning I even checked the show I heard against the TV schedule, and it all matches up. And he practically had a heart attack when he heard about the murders, too."

"You said he was a good actor," Greg pointed out.

"Nobody's that good," Lucy replied.

"That's what I thought about you," Slocum told her.

She smiled. "Thanks."

"It's not a compliment. It's evidence that you can't trust people who are good actors."

"Maybe *you* can't. I was in acting school — that's who I dealt with all day long."

"Anyway, he can't be in two places at once," Greg said.

"Right. So the other stuff doesn't matter anyway," Slocum agreed.

Lucy continued. "You've probably figured out a lot of the details by now. Lucas sent you the pig postcard, I snuck into the dolphin pool area during the trainer's lunch hour, and the stuff with the dolphins was bullshit. Et cetera."

"That doesn't explain all the amazing coincidences that kept coming up," Slocum said.

"Lucas played detective for a long time before we started conning you. He knew things about you that even you don't know. We used to practice weaving them into conversations."

"How cozy."

"It was work, that's all. I never liked the guy. He gives me the creeps," Lucy stated.

Slocum turned to Greg. "What do you think? Is this more horseshit or what?"

"I've got to admit, it sounds more like what."

"What?"

"Exactly."

"Huh?"

"He's on second."

Lucy broke in. "Are you guys always like this?"

"Like what?" Greg asked.

"Well, your friend's on the run for a couple of murders, and you're doing Abbott and Costello routines."

"So?"

She shook her head. "Never mind."

"He's on third," Greg told her.

"So you believe her?" Slocum asked again.

"Yeah. I do."

"Me too. I wish I didn't," Slocum replied.

"Why's that?" Lucy asked.

"It makes everything more complicated."

"But at least you're not in the clutches of some evil temptress," she pointed out.

"No, not an evil one."

Lucy blushed, obscuring several hundred freckles.

Slocum pointed at her. "She can do that on command," he told Greg.

"But this time's real!" Lucy protested.

"Sure. Anyway, Lucas or his boss could still turn up any time now."

"I doubt it. Lucas told me to stay wherever I wanted, so I got this sublet, but getting near the Mystery Spot seems to freak him out, so he only ever visited once. We used to meet at the Holiday Inn."

"Why do you suppose the Mystery Spot bothered him?" Greg asked.

"I can't imagine," Lucy answered.

"I can," Slocum told them. "Lucas' real name is Marcus Beecham and he actually is a heavyweight spiritual figure. He works with energy somehow. And the Spot is probably some sort of real phenomenon that he's sensitive to."

"Whoa," Greg exclaimed. "You're getting just a little wacky on us, partner."

"How do you know all that?" Lucy asked.

"Saddhu Ramba told me. And *there's* a guy whose word you don't have to doubt."

"Yeah?" Greg was skeptical.

"I'm sure of it. There's more too. Lucas/Marcus used to be an ear, nose, and throat specialist. So he would know how to kill people with acupuncture needles. And Lucas, Baba, Saddhu, and some others were all over in India together fifteen years ago. They were followers of some super-heavyweight guru named Brahmachari."

"Really?" Lucy asked. "This doesn't fit my sense of Lucas at all."

"Saddhu said Lucas was a master at working with illusion," Slocum told her.

"I almost wish I'd met the guy too," Greg commented.

"No you don't," Slocum told him. "You're the guy who talked me into this and I still wouldn't wish it on you."

"You're right. Thanks."

"I've got another question," Slocum said to Lucy. "Why does it smell like pizza in here?"

She grinned again. "That's an easy one. I had pizza last night and this morning for breakfast too. There's still quite a bit left. Would anyone like some?" That was the end of conversation for a while.

Eighteen

Slocum wanted Lucy to go to the police and tell them everything. It seemed to him that if she stepped forward, he'd be off the hook. Lucy, however, pointed out that the empty hook would promptly hoist a new candidate into the forefront of the investigation — her. She was sorry Slocum was on the run for something he didn't do, but she wasn't willing to switch places with him.

"I'm not Mother Theresa," was the way she put it. "Indirectly, I've been in cahoots with an apparent murderer. You believe I'm innocent because you know Lucas — I mean Marcus. Do you think the police are going to buy it?"

"Probably not," he admitted. "But you owe me, Lucy."

"The name's Vanessa. And I'm willing to help you — up to a point. I brought you here, didn't I? I could get in big trouble for this."

"I'm sticking with Lucy and Lucas," Slocum replied. "I can't keep up with all this name changing. And I know you're helping me. It's just not enough."

"It's all you're getting." She crossed her arms and glared at him from across the pizza debris on the table.

Greg spoke up. "Suppose we just drag you down there? There's two of us and we're very manly."

"Manly?" Slocum echoed.

"I'll just clam up or tell them you kidnapped me," she asserted.

"But you do think we're manly, right? That's the important thing."

"Well, sure. Very manly."

"I think we're getting a little off the topic," Slocum pointed out.

"Maybe you're right," Greg replied. "What is the topic, anyway?"

"My ass."

"Oh yeah. So what are we going to do about it?"

"Well, I still like the idea of tracking down information about Brahmachari and his disciples," Slocum told him.

"At the bookstore?"

"Yeah. That seems like our best bet."

"I've got an idea," Lucy said. "Lucas reads every word in the newspaper every day. Don't ask me why, but he does."

"So?"

"So we could run a personal ad or something like that and he'd see it. Lucas is the one who could really straighten all this out."

"Or screw it up worse," Slocum responded.

"What could be worse?"

"More bodies?" Greg suggested.

"I don't even know," Slocum admitted. "But he's really powerful and he's really weird and that's not a combination I'm comfortable with right now.

"Okay," Lucy conceded. "But keep it in mind for later."

"Sure."

They decided that Greg would take Lucy's car into town to "commence his gumshoe career," as Greg phrased it. Slocum would catch up on his sleep, while Lucy planned to take Karma for a walk up to the ridge top.

Lying fully clothed on Lucy's baby blue comforter, Slocum was asleep in about five minutes.

He dreamt that he was standing on a narrow beach, with rock cliffs behind him and a perfectly placid, amazingly blue sea before him. Someone called his name from the top of the cliff. It was his father, wearing a yellow hard hat and work clothes. Then another voice called from the other direction. Lucas was standing on the water, about ten yards out.

"Come on," he shouted. "Come on out!"

"I can't walk on water," Slocum called back.

"Sure you can. It's easy."

Slocum took a few tentative steps and it worked. With the next step, though, he plunged underwater and began sinking, no matter how much he flailed or kicked. Down and down he went; the ocean was incredibly deep. He noticed he could breathe, but it was through his ears instead of his nose or mouth. Finally he landed feet first on the bottom. The water was crystal clear and a fat, bald East Indian man sat on a simple wooden throne in front of him.

"Who are you?" Slocum asked. His words were only slightly garbled from being underwater.

There was a pause and then he heard a gentle voice in his head. "Don't be impatient. If you push, you get lies," the telepathic voice said. And fiery red letters spelled out the message above the man's head as well.

Slocum wondered how there could be fire in the ocean. Everything else seemed natural and normal.

Suddenly he was on top of the cliff behind the beach. His dad was hugging him and his face was pressed against his dad's chest. Then Slocum started to cry. It was different than regular crying — more profound. He wasn't sad, exactly. It felt like a release of something — a purge. But it also felt like he'd never stop. He became scared that he was going to cry forever, and he began moaning and wailing.

His dad grabbed him and shook him and then Lucy was shaking him and his eyes opened and he was awake. The tears continued to stream out as he clutched Lucy, burying his face in her neck.

She held him tightly, stroking his hair as he sobbed and gasped. "It was just a bad dream," she told him in a soothing voice. "Everything's okay."

Slocum pressed his face into her clavicle and continued to leak salty tears onto her tee shirt. Gradually, he began calming down. The sobs turned into ragged breaths and the tears slowed.

"Can you keep holding me?" he asked when he could.

"Sure." She maneuvered them into a more comfortable position, lying beside each other on the bed. This time, Slocum's head rested on her bosom; he could hear her heart.

A few tears continued to squeeze out as Slocum took long, deep breaths. Lucy stroked his back and told him again that everything was all right. After a while she asked if he wanted to talk about it. Slocum shook his head, his ear rubbing against one breast and then the other.

Suddenly, he was extremely conscious of his physical proximity to this beautiful woman. He could smell her, feel her against him, and was even being warmed by her nearness. It was intoxicating.

Just then, Lucy kissed him on the top of the head and wriggled. Slocum's favorite organ responded, swelling more with each pulse until it eventually lodged against Lucy's leg.

"Oh my. We *are* feeling better, aren't we?" she commented. But she didn't push him away or loosen her grip.

Slocum began to move his head in slow circles between her breasts. It wasn't something he'd planned; he just discovered himself doing it. His hands pulled her even closer and she slid down, aligning her groin against his swollen member. Their faces were now only a few inches away. Slocum was conscious of his running nose and wet cheeks as he looked into her green eyes.

"I'm a mess," he apologized. "All I seem to do is cry."

She kissed him on the lips and all other concerns slipped away. There was a whole world in that kiss — a sizzling merged realm where everything seemed possible. Slocum's involuntary smile reformed the shape of the kiss, and then he closed his eyes and fell further into sexual oblivion.

Later, their coupling was equally dramatic. If Slocum's previous sexual experiences could be likened to fireworks, this was a full-fledged thunderstorm — primal and awe inspiring. There was some kind of chemistry or energy between Lucy and Slocum that he'd never encountered before. Sensation, emotion, and sexual response were all heightened and rendered clearer somehow. It was truly wonderful. Lucy didn't even become irate when he fell asleep afterwards.

* * *

Awakening was a rude transition. All of Slocum's aches and pains, virtually forgotten during the love-making, screamed at his emerging consciousness. There wasn't even anyone to complain to, Lucy and Karma were gone. Slocum limped into the shower, and despite his pain, savored the experience of becoming clean. Unwilling to don Junior's crusty oversized clothes, he threw on Lucy's white terrycloth robe, which almost fit.

There was no mirror in the bathroom, but Lucy had hung a small one behind the kitchen sink. Slocum was shocked to see his battered face. The cut over his eye was a nasty red worm with jagged edges. Under his substantial dark stubble, one cheek was scraped raw. The other one was so badly bruised that it resembled a hairy, overripe plum. His bloodshot eyes displayed a haunted expression and puffy dark pouches underlined the effect.

Basically, he looked like a murderer on the run. He was so absorbed in his self-examination that he didn't hear Greg drive up. When his friend opened the front door, he whirled, placed too much weight on his sprained ankle, and toppled. Slocum grabbed a plastic chair on his way down, thus allowing himself to experience both the pain of landing on the hard wooden floor, and the considerable discomfort of the chair falling on his shin.

Greg applauded. "Splendid. Very spectacular."

"Just shut up and help me up."

He did, placing two hardcover books and a grocery bag on the white table to free his hands. They sat at the table after Greg fetched two more beers from the small fridge.

"Where are the gals?" Greg asked. He was wearing jeans, Birkenstocks, and a green sweatshirt.

"I don't know. I've been asleep. What time is it, anyway?"

"About five. Sorry I took so long, but I stopped and bought you some new secondhand clothes at Goodwill."

"New secondhand ones, huh?"

"Yup. Look." He pulled a mostly orange Hawaiian shirt from the grocery bag. Purple surfers rode the crests of yellow waves on it.

"Very tasteful," Slocum commented, sipping his beer.

"Hey, they don't smell like something died in them. I didn't have much money."

The pants, at least, were basic brown corduroy Levis that almost fit. Slocum changed into his new ensemble as Greg filled him in on his research expedition.

"First of all, let me say that those Cruz Mountain people are very weird. This woman clerk who looked like a transvestite

George Bush on drugs talked my ear off for about twenty minutes about her trip to India. I swear she must've had every digestive disorder known to mankind. But anyway I found two really good books. One is by Brahmachari and the other one is about him by... guess who?"

"Uh... Lucas?"

"Baba Ahimsa. He was Brahmachari's secretary. All the inner circle of disciples had specific duties over there."

"Does it name names?" Fully dressed, Slocum plopped down into one of the white plastic kitchen chairs.

"Even better. There's a group photo. Let me find it." Greg leafed through a thick green volume. "There!" He passed the book to Slocum, who looked at it and dropped it on the table in shock. Brahmachari sat on a simple wooden throne just as he had in Slocum's dream.

"Whoa!"

"What?" Greg asked. "What's the big deal?"

"I just dreamt about this guy."

"Who? Brahmachari?"

Slocum nodded. His heart was racing. It wasn't as though Lucas was on hand pulling some crap on him. This was real.

"Calm down," Greg told his friend. "Probably you've seen a photo of the guy before."

"No, I haven't."

"You wouldn't necessarily remember. It could have been embedded in your unconscious."

"Yeah, maybe. Let me see that picture again." He retrieved the book and studied the photograph. A few moments later he was absorbed in an examination of the super-guru's disciples. Standing behind the throne were six people, fanned out in a semicircle. Slocum recognized Lucas, Baba Ahimsa, and Saddhu Ramba. Although the picture was sixteen years old, they all looked about the same as he remembered them. There was also a beautiful Indian woman, a man who looked as though he was either Tibetan or some sort of South American Indian, and an older man who was clearly Chinese. Brahmachari dominated the scene, though.

He had been a very large man with a huge belly. He wore only a white loincloth. His facial expression was a study in fierceness. Brahmachari looked more like a tribal chieftain than a spiritual leader.

"What was Lucas' job?" Slocum asked after another swig of beer.

"Security."

"That figures. How about Saddhu?"

"He taught the new students at the ashram. They seemed to have been mostly Europeans."

"Maybe we ought to check into these three other people in the photo," Slocum suggested.

"I'm way ahead of you, Bro. The woman's dead. Natural causes about six years ago. The Tibetan guy is named Rinpoche Tilopa. Well, actually that's like his title, but it's what he goes by. The Chinese dude is really old now and they don't trust him down at the bookstore. His name is Feng Shi. But here's the interesting part. Rinpoche and Feng both live in Santa Cruz too."

"I knew about Feng, but how did you find out all the rest?"

"From Ms. Bush the store clerk. And some other books I couldn't afford. It seems that Brahmachari instructed everyone about where he wanted them to live. I don't know why."

"Remind me to pay you back," Slocum said.

"I will. And next time I'm wanted for murder, I'll expect full reciprocity."

Slocum smiled. "It's a deal."

"I found out a few more things too," Greg added. "Rinpoche was in charge of the meditation program at Brahmachari's place, and now he runs a Buddhist monastery back in the hills near Felton."

"Buddhist? I figured all these people were Hindus."

"No. Brahmachari wasn't associated with any particular crowd, although a lot of his followers were. The Indian woman was a Zoroastrian because she was actually Persian, even though she was born in India. And Feng Shi is associated with something Chinese that has a lot of martial arts in it. I can't remember the name of it. But he also has a kung-fu school up on Mission Street that's for anybody willing to shell out the bucks for classes. He has a reputation for being ambitious and sort of violent for a spiritual guy."

"Kind of like Lucas, maybe," Slocum told him. "This is a lot more than I thought we'd find out, not that it really solves anything."

"Wait. I'm not done. In his book, Brahmachari says that he is to be succeeded by one of his inner circle someday. And the book you've got says that he called them all in when he was on his deathbed. But nobody knows what he said. I mean the people that were there know, but they've kept it a secret."

"Jesus. This just gets more and more complicated. Do you understand...."

"Wait a minute," Greg interrupted. "I think I hear a car."

The door burst open, revealing an ordinary-looking middle-aged man dressed in a gray suit and a red tie. The gun in his hand wasn't ordinary.

"Freeze, gents."

Behind him, the dirt roadway was littered with yellow Ford Escorts.

"You're from Cruz Mountain, aren't you?" Slocum asked.

"You bet your ass," the man told them. "Lie on the floor — hands on your head."

"Okay. No problem." As they moved to comply, several more people strode into the house. Then Slocum and Greg were face-down and someone was tying their hands behind them.

"How'd you find us?" Slocum asked.

"Your friend here," a woman answered. "It wasn't too smart for him to come into our bookstore."

"Shit," Greg muttered.

Next, someone was placing bags over their heads. "So you're going to turn us in to the police?" Slocum managed to ask before being bagged.

"Hell no," a man's voice answered. "We're going to find out about those damn walls — or else."

Nineteen

After very uncomfortable rides on the floorboards of their respective Escorts, Slocum and Greg were reunited, led into a building, and then ushered down a flight of creaky stairs. Hands untied their rope bonds and then removed the paper bags from their heads. A harsh glare from fluorescent lighting greeted their eyes. As Slocum's pupils adjusted, he glimpsed the backs of a woman and a man ascending a wood staircase in a corner of the basement. The man with the gun stood on the other side of a full-sized pool table from his two prisoners. The felt on the table was bright green and perfectly clean. The man was just as ordinary-looking as he had appeared to be at Lucy's.

He could've been a mid-level insurance executive nearing the end of his career or maybe a furniture store owner. The only remarkable thing about him was the placement of his ears, which were unevenly rooted on the sides of his head. The left one was probably an inch and a half lower than the right. The net effect was an impression that one of the ears had slid down, perhaps because it had been shoddily affixed in the first place.

"You'll be staying here for a while," the man told them, waving the small revolver carelessly.

"Oh goodie," Greg replied.

The man with the gun — now held tightly and aimed at the vicinity of Slocum's gut — tried to stare Greg down. Greg smiled back at him.

The man turned to Slocum. "You'd better tell your friend that this is a very serious situation."

"This is a very serious situation, Greg."

"Oh, thanks. Sometimes I get so mixed up. I thought it was an opportunity to shoot pool for free." He spoke to their captor next. "That's certainly worth dying for, don't you think?"

The man shook his head and departed up the stairs.

"Let's explore," Slocum suggested.

"Look for a bathroom first."

"Right."

They were in a basement built of cinder blocks. The walls and ceiling were white; a brown shag carpet covered a slab concrete floor. There was a small bathroom, which Greg promptly used, but there were no windows. Other than the pool table, there was a dart board with no darts, an old black vinyl couch, and a yellow plastic wall clock with a happy face design. The door at the top of the stairs was the only way out. Of course it was securely locked from the other side.

"It's kind of demeaning to be held prisoner in a rec room," Slocum complained from where he'd settled down onto the couch.

Greg was collecting the billiard balls from the table's leather pockets, gathering them at one end of the table. His sweatshirt was almost exactly the same color as the felt.

"I know what you mean, but at least we've got something to do."

"That's true. Best out of eleven billion eight ball games?"

"You're on."

While they played, they discussed their situation and tried to figure out how to free themselves. Immediately, a series of questions confronted them. Would these people believe Slocum if he told them the truth about the walls and Baba? Were they planning to turn him in to the police? Did they represent the entire Cruz Mountain community or were they a radical splinter group? Was the one gun they'd seen the only gun? How willing were these so-called spiritual people to actually shoot someone? Why were they waiting to do whatever they were going to do next?

To a large degree, any escape plans that Slocum and Greg concocted had to be based on the answers to such questions. If the gun was a prop, that was one thing. If the man with the gun was fully prepared to use it, that was an entirely different situation.

So they reasoned, and guessed, and shot pool, and re-explored the rec room. Eventually, they settled on a plan and readied themselves to implement it.

They'd been prisoners for about three hours when Slocum rapped on the basement door. After a moment, light footsteps approached it from the other side.

"Yeah?" It was a woman's voice.

"I'm ready to negotiate," Slocum told her.

"What do you mean?"

"I'll cut a deal for the information you want."

"Hold on." The footsteps retraced their route. After a minute or two they returned.

"No," the woman told him.

"What do you mean, 'no'? Do you want to find out about the walls or not?"

"We're not ready to talk to you yet. Just wait until we come get you."

"It's got to be now. My friend's in the bathroom and he doesn't share my point of view."

"So?"

"Look, lady. I'm trying...."

"Hold on," she interrupted. Then Slocum heard her calling in the other direction. "Is he here? What should I do?" She left again but in just a minute several sets of footsteps approached the basement.

"Get away from the door," an elderly male voice called.

"Okay." Slocum limped to the bottom of the staircase.

The door opened and the well-dressed man with the gun came through, followed by an old, black-bearded man who looked like an Eastern Orthodox priest, and a clean-cut young man dressed in navy blue athletic sweats.

"Where's the other guy?" the elderly man asked as the threesome climbed down into the basement. His tone of voice was sharp. Everything about him was intense, in fact. He projected a ruthlessness that was unusual in someone his age. He must've been seventy-five or eighty.

His eyes were dark brown and didn't blink as often as normal. He had a sharply hooked nose and very large, red lips. He made quite an impression; he wasn't even slightly ordinary looking, unless you counted a brown 1970s style leisure suit as ordinary.

"He's in the bathroom," Slocum reported as he leaned against the pool table.

The man snapped his fingers and gestured to the young man, who prowled around the room, even glancing under the pool table.

"He's in the bathroom all right," he reported in a soft voice.

"Let's make this fast," Slocum suggested. "My friend and I don't see eye to eye on this thing."

The old man stood in front of Slocum; the other two fanned out behind him.

"First things first," the bearded man said. "I've got some news that complicates all this." His voice was commanding.

"What?"

"Rinpoche Tilopa has been murdered too."

Slocum moved over to the couch and fell onto it. "Jesus."

"How'd it happen?" the man with the gun asked. He sounded very shocked. "Wasn't he taking precautions?"

"He was," the old man replied. "It was a rifle shot."

"Jesus," Slocum repeated.

"At the monastery?" the gun man asked.

The old man nodded. "Two hours ago. Whoever did it got away."

"Two hours ago?" Slocum asked. "While I've been locked up in here?"

The old man nodded again. "We know now that you're not the murderer, assuming the murders are connected, which is pretty obvious. It was Feng Shi, I guess. He's a very bitter man."

"Great! So let us go, huh?"

"There's still the matter of the walls, and the fact that we're your alibi. Why should we admit that we've held you captive?"

"Hmm. Good point." While Slocum thought it through, the man with the gun spoke up.

"Your friend is taking an awful lot of time in there," he said.

"Huh? Oh, he has diarrhea. Look it, how about this?" he offered. "If I cooperate with you, we'll just say we were visiting or talking while the Tibetan guy was killed. That way, you get your information and I get my alibi."

"Why are you willing to tell us now when you wouldn't before?"

"Let's just say things are different. An experience like this can change someone, you know."

"True enough," the man conceded.

"So we have a deal?"

The old man strode forward and held out his hand. "What about the gun?" Slocum asked.

The man with the gun looked to his leader for direction.

"Show him," was the older man's response.

"It's not loaded," he told Slocum, spinning the empty cylinder and placing it on the pool table.

"Come on out, Greg," Slocum called as he grasped the old man's hand.

The Cruz Mountain contingent turned to the bathroom door; Greg dropped down from where he'd been wedged just under the pool table's slate top. His pockets were filled with billiard balls and a strip of torn tee shirt material held most of a pool cue secure against his back.

"The Cue Commando will wait and fight another day," Greg announced. He divested himself of his crude weapons and joined Slocum on the couch as the others gaped at him.

"There's just one thing," Slocum told them. "I'm not sure you guys would really want to hear what Baba said if you knew what it was."

"What do you mean?"

"Well, suppose he told me that the walls were foundations for fast food restaurants or cheesy condominiums. Would you really want to know?"

"It couldn't possibly have been anything like that," the man who'd had the gun protested.

"How about I tell it to one person that you guys designate, and then he or she can decide whether to pass it on to everyone else?" Slocum suggested.

"Fine," the elderly man replied. Without discussion, his two compatriots left the room. "What about your friend?" the old man asked. "Does he know?"

"No."

"Then why doesn't he stay in the bathroom while we talk?"

Slocum agreed and Greg left the room.

"So?" The man roosted on the edge of the pool table and waited. His fierceness had softened but he was still a formidable conversation partner. His thick black beard was like the ones on Assyrian statues — so stylized in its curl structure that it almost didn't look real.

"The last thing I asked Baba was why y'all were building the walls," Slocum told him.

"Yes?"

"He wrote 'I don't know' and laughed."

The man's face visibly drooped and for the first time he appeared to be just another elderly soul putting in his time.

"Now I understand," he intoned morosely.

"Can I come out yet?" Greg shouted from the bathroom.

"No! We'll call you when we're done," Slocum yelled back.

"This is a difficult situation indeed," the old man commented, gazing down at his clasped hands.

"If it's any consolation, I didn't get the impression that there wasn't any reason — just that Baba didn't know what it was. And not knowing it didn't seem to bother him."

"You don't understand our situation," the man told him. "And there's no point in trying to explain it."

The door to the basement opened and seven or eight people, including the two who had just left, paraded down the stairs.

They were all obviously uncomfortable about something.

"What's going on?" the leader demanded.

"Hello Mel!" a voice boomed from the end of the line. The shotgun in his hand preceded Lucas into the room.

Twenty

"Marcus!" the old man exclaimed.

"In the flesh, my friend. Marcus to the rescue."

Greg opened the bathroom door a crack, scoped out the situation, and closed it again.

"Now unhand my friend there. Are you alright, Slocum?"

He nodded. Things had once again moved faster than he could immediately handle. Lucas/Marcus was wearing his usual outfit, jeans, a light blue workshirt, and brown boots. His long hair was tied back in a ponytail. He held the single barrel shotgun much too familiarly to suit Slocum. And why was he smiling? You don't smile when you're threatening people.

The room was full of bodies now; most of them were packed into the back of the room, behind the pool table.

"You look old, Mel," Lucas said. "Are you in charge now?"

"It hasn't been decided," the old man responded. "But I'm afraid you're laboring under a misunderstanding concerning our young friend. We've negotiated an agreement and he's free to go."

"That's right," Slocum agreed, recovering his wits. "Greg got away hours ago and when Mel got here and he and I had a chance to talk, we found out we didn't have any problems."

"Well, so much the better," Lucas replied smoothly. "I'll give you a lift."

"Actually, I was going to help Mel with something here," Slocum said.

"Lucy and that particularly hirsute canine she has acquired are waiting outside, Slocum. You wouldn't want to disappoint them, would you?"

"Maybe I could meet you guys later," he tried.

"Lucy's going to the police if we don't emerge in..." Lucas checked his watch, "...four minutes."

"Really?"

"Absolutely." The conviction was total. In the one word was all the weight that one man could collect in a lifetime.

Strangely, it wasn't enough to budge Slocum. "I think I'll stay here," he announced, crossing his arms.

Lucas hefted the shotgun absent-mindedly. "That won't do. We need to talk; I know who the murderer is. And Lucy's waiting."

Slocum stood, rooted.

Mel spoke up. "It's Feng, isn't it?" he asked.

"Yes," Lucas replied. "He's been setting me up for months." He looked at Slocum. "Do you need a demonstration of what this gun can do?"

"Uh, no. I'm familiar with shotguns. My dad hunted."

"Then I suggest you get moving, my friend."

Hardly noticing his sore ankle, Slocum scooted across the room and up the stairs. His mind a blank, he wandered through the house trying to find his way out. Eventually, Lucas found him and led him out. They were in an expensive neighborhood that Slocum didn't recognize. It was dark out; it might've been eight or nine p.m. Lucas' black truck was parked on the front lawn. Lucy sat in the cab and Karma lay in the truck bed.

"I was just about to give up," Lucy told them as they piled in the cab. "Oh Slocum, I'm so glad you're okay."

She sat between the two men. Lucas was behind the wheel, the shotgun by his side. Slocum was pressed against the passenger door in an effort to distance himself from the others. His rayon Hawaiian shirt rubbed uncomfortably on the back of his neck.

"Was this your idea?" he asked Lucy belligerently.

"Well, sort of. Karma and I got back in time to see those silly yellow cars leave. I was afraid they'd turn you into the police or something. So when Lucas called, I told him about the cars and he knew all about them and where you might be. So I talked him into going in after you. There wasn't any violence, was there?"

"Not quite. Lucas decided not to shoot me."

By now, the truck was exiting the Pasatiempo Country Club and turning south on Graham Hill Road back towards downtown.

"What do you mean?" Lucy asked.

"Ask your friend."

"Lucas?"

"I did what was best. We can sort it out later," he replied.

"Did you remember to bring those books?"

"Yes."

There was a pause. Slocum suspected it was purely for dramatic effect. Then Lucas spoke again.

"When we get to my motel, Slocum, give me a half hour of your time. If you wish to leave then — fine."

"All right," Slocum agreed, mostly based on the general principle of avoiding conflicts that might end in gunfire.

Just before they arrived at the Eiffel Tower Motel, down on the edge of Beach Flats, Slocum asked Lucy how Karma was doing.

"Oh she's fine. She's just the biggest sweetheart. I don't think I've ever met a nicer dog."

"Did she like Lucas?"

"It's funny you should ask that," Lucy replied. "She didn't take to him much — just wagged once and then seemed to lose interest."

"I'm more of a cat person," Lucas explained as Slocum filed away the dog barometer information, although he couldn't make up his mind how much weight to assign to a canine reference.

The motel was incredibly ugly. An eight-foot-tall Eiffel Tower made of yellow fiberglass squatted on the flat roof of the motel office. It was lit by red spotlights, which turned it into an indeterminate muddy color. The color scheme of the building was red, white and blue, except the doors of the rooms which were black, with the room numbers in gold glitter. The motel was three blocks from the Main Beach, but only a block from where the major drug deals in town went down. No one but a particularly dumb tourist or a shotgun-toting guru would select the Eiffel Tower Motel.

Although there were only a couple of dozen rooms, Lucas' was number 479. Lucy carried in the two books that Greg had bought; Lucas left the gun in the truck. Karma decided to go in too. The interior decor boggled the mind. It looked as if a poorer, more audacious Elvis had decorated it. Everything was grossly overdone, including larger than life oil paintings of kittens, and an elaborate plastic chandelier with candle-shaped bulbs.

"It's a slice of Americana," Lucas pronounced. "Sit anywhere."

Karma promptly jumped up onto one of the twin beds and encamped on top of the pillow.

"That's why I'm a cat person," Lucas said.

Slocum and Lucy sat in the two green velour-covered armchairs near the door and Lucas stood in front of them.

"Basically," he began, stroking his multi-colored beard, "I want to apologize for my role in this debacle. We've all been manipulated by a maestro, and believe me, if someone can pull *my* strings, they're no slouch." He moved to a parade rest posture, his legs spread with his hands behind him. "I trusted Feng Shi. He was one of Brahmachari's inner circle and I assumed that helping to fulfill his goals was helping mankind itself."

"He's the killer?" Lucy asked.

Lucas pulled a cassette tape out of his shirt pocket and handed it to Lucy. She examined it and passed it to Slocum. It was a commercial recording entitled "Feng Shi Talks: Carmel, 1989." Slocum returned it to Lucas, who popped it in a portable tape player sitting on top of a low bureau.

"So we find that the meaning of this expression is very similar to that...."

"That's him!" Lucy exclaimed. Lucas shut off the machine.

"That's the guy that gave us orders over the phone," she explained to Slocum. "Remember — the guy with the complicated accent?"

Slocum nodded. "Tell us more," he said to Lucas.

"Have you seen the photograph in the book?" the guru asked.

"Yes. If you mean the one over in India with Brahmachari."

"Exactly. One of us is destined to carry on his work, and now there's only Feng Shi, me, and Rinpoche Tilopa left."

Slocum shook his head. "Rinpoche was shot today. He's dead too."

"Oh no," Lucy gasped.

Lucas' eyes narrowed. "I thought he'd be okay at the monastery. I warned him, but it never occurred to me that Shi would use a gun. It's a complete betrayal of all he stands for — stood for, I should say."

"Why wouldn't he use a gun?" Slocum asked.

"He's a healer, a martial artist, and an advocate for charity above all else. Does that answer your question?"

"Yes. But you're not making much of a case against him by pointing all that out."

Lucas shrugged and the gesture seemed totally alien to him, as if he'd never done it before. "How's this, my friend? Shi was an acupuncturist for many years. He even wrote a book on it that I've got somewhere." He turned and rummaged through a duffel bag at the foot of Karma's bed. She farted loudly.

"That's another reason why I'm a cat person," Lucas said. "Ah, here it is." He held up the book. The cover was mostly white with black lettering. *Secrets of the Masters: The Vertebrae Points* was the title, and Feng Shi was listed as the author.

"Why'd you tell me you were an anesthesiologist?" Slocum asked.

Lucas put the book down. "Shi told me to. I see now that a great deal of his directions were designed to frame you to the police, and also to convince you that I was the real murderer."

"So he's covered either way?" Lucy asked.

"Exactly. If the police buy the frame, then they settle for Slocum. If they don't, then I'm the next framee, so to speak. And given your experiences, Slocum, a very likely candidate indeed."

"Once I was in jail and the killing continued, it would've been obvious that they had the wrong man," Slocum pointed out.

"That's true," Lucas conceded. "I hadn't thought that part through. So Shi planned from the start to frame us both in sequence, and your escaping from the police prevented him from shifting the blame onto me. By the way, how did you escape?"

"It turns out I have friends in low places."

Lucy grinned and Lucas looked puzzled.

"And how did Greg get away from the Cruz Mountain contingent?" he asked.

"They weren't very competent kidnappers," Slocum replied.

"I've got a question," Lucy announced.

"Shoot," Slocum responded.

"No, it's for Lucas. I want to run something back to see if I've got it straight."

"Shoot," Lucas replied, awkwardly pronouncing the borrowed word.

"There are two people left from Brahmachari's inner circle, right?"

Lucas nodded, his eyes pinned to hers.

"And you're saying that one of them is a mass murderer." She paused and Lucas nodded again.

"So the other one has to be Brahmachari's successor. When you say Feng Shi's the killer, you're also saying *you're* the one who's inheriting some huge spiritual responsibility. Am I right?"

"Yes. That's it. I don't feel any different, but I must be the one," Lucas told her.

"Suppose neither of you is the killer," Slocum posited.

"How can that be?" Lucy asked.

"Hey," Slocum answered. "If I was used by you, and you were used by Lucas, and he was used by Feng Shi, then who's to say he couldn't have been used by somebody? What's the difference if the chain goes up four spots or five?"

"But who?" Lucy asked.

"I don't know."

"And why?" Lucas responded. "That's the real question. Who else could possibly have a motive for murdering some of the most saintly beings on this planet?"

"Hey, John Hinkley shot Reagan to impress Jodie Foster. There are a lot of very sick people out there," Slocum replied. "And I'm not so clear on Feng Shi's motive anyway. Why would a guy like that flip out? Just to inherit a job or whatever that's all about?"

"I can help with that," Lucas answered. "We're not talking about a job here, Slocum. I can't go into it in any detail, but Brahmachari's legacy entails immense power. Enough to corrupt? Well, the facts speak for themselves."

"Suppose *you* were the one who set up a double frame," Slocum remarked. "Suppose you wanted a back-up fall guy in case the cops didn't go for me, or I didn't get nabbed or something. You could've constructed the whole thing so that suspicion would fall on Feng Shi next."

"There are several reasons why that doesn't make sense, Slocum. I'll bet Lucy can name a few."

"I can," she agreed. "For one thing, there was Feng Shi's voice telling us what to do over the phone. And then Lucas was on the phone with me when Saddhu Ramba was killed. You know all this, Slocum."

"Maybe you're the murderer," Slocum suggested to her.

"Slocum," Lucy's eyes were emerald daggers.

"Hey, it was just a thought. If you were talking to Lucas, he was talking to you, anyway."

"Yeah." Lucy was irate.

"Calm down, calm down. I'm just trying to be thorough." There was a pause of several seconds while Slocum assembled his next thought. "This ought to be an easy one to call. One guy is supposed to be the new messiah or something and the other one's practically the devil incarnate. The only thing worse would be offing Mother Theresa, and who knows — maybe she's on the list. So why do I have to stop and think about this? Something's screwy here."

"Perhaps I can help," Lucas suggested. "There's a level of spiritual attainment which transcends ordinary morality. Brahmachari, for example, used to hit beggars that ventured too close to him. In the rarified atmosphere of Saddhus and Gurus, it's much harder to tell who's who than in the general population. Here's another example. There's a story in India about a young disciple who seeks guidance from his Master. The Master tells him to go live in the middle of the highway. So he does, and years go by. He tries to get used to life in the middle of the highway, without his Master, but it's hard. Periodically he loses his temper or lusts after a comely female traveler. Finally, after ten long years, a soldier on horseback comes along the road and halts in front of the disciple.

"'Move!' shouts the soldier. 'I will go around no man.'

"The disciple's immense frustration suddenly bursts forth. He leaps to his feet, grabs the man's sword and hacks him to pieces. Aghast at what he's done, he collapses in a heap, sobbing. His Master appears by his side.

"'You have done well,' he tells the disciple. 'That man was on his way to give the execution order for one hundred innocent men in the next village. The king will not send another soldier and all one hundred will live.'" Lucas sat on the edge of the bed when he'd finished.

"Say what?" Slocum responded.

"I think I get it," Lucy said.

Lucas gestured for her to continue.

"The truly high people know so much more than everybody else that you can't judge them."

"That's about the size of it," Lucas agreed. As usual, his delivery of a common phrase sounded odd.

"You know," Slocum interjected. "I just remembered a dream I had recently. It had Brahmachari in it, but I'd never seen a picture of him or anything until afterwards in these books."

Lucas was suddenly very alert. "Did he speak?"

"Yes. Although I understand he didn't in real life."

"What did he say? Try to use the exact words. This could be very important."

"He said 'Don't be impatient. If you push, you get lies,'" Slocum reported.

Lucas' fingers began wriggling and twitching, and his head began bobbing as well. It was hard for him to force words out.

"That's all... for tonight. Let's meet... at nine in the morning...at Lucy's." His eyes closed and he was somewhere else.

"Come on," Lucy said. "My car's around the corner. We can crash at my place." She grabbed the books and opened the door.

"Does he do that a lot?" Slocum asked.

" *I've* never seen it."

Karma hopped off the bed and followed them out the door.

"And he was acting so normal there for a while," Slocum commented. "He was really doing great."

Lucy took his hand. "We'll work this out, Sloke."

"Sloke?"

"You'll get used to it."

"Oh boy."

Twenty-One

After a night of love-making, deep sleep, more love making, conversation, and not so deep sleep, Slocum was awakened by a rapping on Lucy's door. Lucy and Karma were gone again.

"Who is it?" he called from the bed.

"The boogie man," Greg told him.

"Come on in."

Greg and Flinch walked in. The homeless man looked especially feral in his olive fatigues.

"I'm here too," Greg said.

It took Flinch a moment to get it, then he elbowed Greg and told him to watch it.

"How'd you get here?" Slocum asked.

"Mel lent me a little yellow car to go save you in," Greg told him. "He doesn't think too much of Marcus, that's for sure."

"I don't either," Flinch added. "The cocksucker."

"So where'd you go instead of saving me?" Slocum asked, sitting up with the sheet around him. Flinch began exploring the cabin.

"The vets' camp. I figured I needed some help so I spent the night up there. The cops never did find it."

"So everybody's okay up there? I'll bet they miss Karma."

"You bet your ass they do," Flinch interjected from the kitchen area. "Buddha Boy wants her back. And Verlin says you should come back and visit when this is all over."

"I will. You guys really put yourselves on the line for me," Slocum told him. "I won't forget it and I hope I have the chance to pay y'all back."

"So how'd you get away from Lucas?" Greg asked.

"Just walked. It wasn't what it looked like — Lucas just wanted to talk and he was pretty convincing."

"About what?"

"That Feng Shi's behind all this."

"The Chinese guy from the photo?"

"Yeah. I'll tell you about it later. What time is it?"

"Around eight. I hope this wasn't an inconvenient time to come save you."

"No, it's ducky. It's just that Lucas is due here at nine and I'd rather that he didn't know about you guys. You can be my ace in the hole."

"Sure," Greg agreed. "Where's Lucy?"

"Out walking the dog, I think."

"Is she straight?" Greg asked.

"She ain't no bull dyke," Flinch answered from the bathroom. "I'd say she and our boy have been getting mighty friendly in their little love nest."

"Shut up, Flinch," Greg told him. "I meant is she honest."

"I think so," Slocum answered. "But why don't you guys split before she gets back, just to be on the safe side. Get the number off the phone and call here at eleven. If I'm not here, I'll meet you somewhere at noon if I can."

"Where?"

"I don't know. I can't go anywhere too public."

"How about the jetty out at the harbor?" Flinch suggested. "We've got wheels. We might as well make it somewhere scenic."

"Okay, fine."

While Greg was checking the phone number, Flinch quizzed him about why Greg wasn't scared of him like everyone else was.

"I don't know, Flinch. There's just something about you that I can't take too seriously."

On the way out the door, Flinch wanted to know what it was. "I can work on it if I know what it is," he was explaining.

Slocum showered and pulled on the clown clothes Greg had selected for him. He was very tired of the Hawaiian shirt by now; it wasn't something you wanted to wake up to.

"I might have a sweater that would fit you," Lucy said from the doorway. Her freckles seemed to be darker and more distinct than usual. Her hair was up on her head in a bun.

Karma trotted in and snuffled his pants leg.

"That would be very, very nice," Slocum replied as he stroked Karma's big, bushy head. "In fact, I'll make you breakfast if you can come up with something."

"Will you pet me like that too?"

"You bet."

So, clad in a green sweater and his brown corduroy Levis, Slocum made enough scrambled eggs for all the people and dogs in the house. Karma got toast too, but there wasn't enough for everyone.

During breakfast, Lucy told Slocum about some things she'd read in the book about Brahmachari.

"When have you had time to read?" Slocum asked.

"While you were off being kidnapped, which by the way was just a little inconsiderate when you think about it."

"Sorry. I don't know what I was thinking."

"Well anyway, shut up and listen," Lucy told him. "Brahmachari was an amazing guy. Do you know that he was sometimes seen in two places at once?"

"Yeah? Who were his witnesses — his mom and dad?"

"Uh-uh. All kinds of people — lawyers for instance, and doctors. Also he could touch people's eyeballs and zap them somehow and then their hearts would get opened up."

"That sounds painful."

"Well they had their eyes closed at the time and believe me nobody ever complained. And get this. One time he didn't eat anything for six months but he didn't lose any weight."

"Do you believe all that?" Slocum asked.

"I don't know. But you're going to have to think about this one. Guess how he worked?"

"I don't know what you mean. Worked at what?"

"How he helped his people and all."

"I have no idea."

"Guess."

"Uh, he gave them teachings on an Etch-a-Sketch?"

"Nope. He appeared in their dreams, Slocum."

"You're kidding."

She shook her head, her eyes open wide. "And he's been doing it since he died too."

Slocum just sat and stared at her.

"It's kind of scary, isn't it?" Lucy commented. "Apparently, he talks to people telepathically in their dreams and the message sometimes appears as bright red writing in the sky too. Is that what your dream was like, Slocum?"

Slocum nodded, hoisted a fork full of eggs to his mouth, and chewed them diligently. "Let's talk about something else," he suggested. His gut felt as though someone had kicked it and his chest was so tight he could hardly breathe. For the first time in his life, he managed to not think of something he was trying not to think of.

"What?"

"Well, Lucas will be here soon. What do you think he wants from us?" Now his face felt weird — as if his expression was frozen in place. He didn't know just which expression it was; he just knew he'd lost the ability to change whichever one it was to another one.

"Help against Feng Shi, I guess. I mean the guy must be gunning for Lucas. He's the last one left. Are you sure you're okay?"

"I don't know, but I really don't want to talk about it." Slocum watched the dog eat for a moment. "What can we do against a kung fu expert, anyway? I'm tempted to just go to the police."

"And tell them what?"

"The whole story from start to finish."

Lucy tilted her head and then propped it up on a fist. "If you feel that's the best thing to do, I'll go along with it. But do you think you can really trust the Cruz Mountain people? I mean even if all they say is that they were talking to you when Rinpoche was shot, they're still admitting they were hanging around with a wanted criminal. Not turning you in has to be some kind of crime, right? The same goes for me and all those homeless men, too. And Greg. How can you tell your story leaving all that out? It's not going to make any sense."

Slocum sighed. "Have you ever noticed how nothing's simple?"

"You know," Lucy replied, "I think that's what spirituality is all about — finding the simple truths that are behind all this hodgepodge."

"Hey, do you have hidden depths or what?"

"I burn with an intense inner fire, actually. It's a Zen thing."

"Great. I like that in a woman."

Slocum was out of his seat and en route to fondling her when he heard someone knock on the door. He glanced at Lucy's alarm clock.

"It's exactly nine. It must be Lucas," he said.

"He's always exactly on time."

Slocum opened the door. Lucas was out of uniform. He wore a brown corduroy sport coat over a white shirt and khaki dress pants. He did have his old boots on though.

"Who is this guy?" Slocum asked Lucy. "Do you know him?"

"I'm in disguise," Lucas told them, and then laughed his deep, liquid laugh.

"Well come on in," Lucy called from the table. "Pull up a chair."

Lucas was still chortling as he sat down. Slocum cleared the table, stacked the dishes in the small stainless steel sink, and then joined the others at the table. His ankle didn't bother him a whole lot any more.

"Well," Lucy began, "Here we are. I guess the Mystery Spot isn't bothering you today."

Lucas acted as though he hadn't heard her. "I've got a plan and I need both of you to implement it," he said. "I'm going to offer myself as bait in an effort to entrap Shi, but I need someone to cover my back, and someone else to call the police at the right moment."

"It sounds dangerous," Lucy responded. "Isn't there some other way?"

"Not that I can think of," Lucas answered. "We need to clear all our names and put the murderer out of commission. There seem to be a very limited number of choices that can accomplish those goals."

"Suppose it turns out that Feng Shi isn't the bad guy? I mean it is a possibility, at least," Slocum pointed out.

"Then we'll have another ally — a very powerful ally — for our next step. We'll have lost nothing and gained a great deal."

Slocum nodded. That was true enough. But if a third party was the killer, he'd have both of the remaining victims on hand. On the other hand, if Lucas was involved in the murders — perhaps indirectly — he'd have his enemy and all the key witnesses gathered together. There seemed to be a lot of ways the cookie could crumble. Slocum remembered Greg and Flinch and momentarily found solace. If he got them involved, maybe he could be ready for any eventuality. On the other hand, Flinch was crazed and Greg steadfastly refused to take anything seriously. A guy could have more reliable aces in his hole.

"I've worked out most of how to set it up," Lucas reported, "but I'm not sure where it ought to happen. We need somewhere fairly dark — I was thinking of scheduling the meeting for ten at night — but there has to be some light. And we need some place a little out of the way, but close enough to the police station so they can get there in a hurry. I don't want it to be hard to find or near any people either, in case there's shooting. Any ideas?"

"The beach?" Lucy tried.

"No cover for you two," Lucas replied.

"The Mystery Spot?" Slocum asked.

"Too far away from the police."

"The wharf?"

"Too public."

"How about one of the earthquaked buildings or lots downtown?"

"Hmm. That's not bad." Lucas stroked his beard. "But we would be right downtown and the police patrol those areas."

"West Cliff?" Lucy suggested.

"The lighthouse!" Slocum exclaimed. "It's perfect."

Lucas pulled back his lips and simulated a smile. "Thank you. It *is* perfect."

"What about a phone? There's no phone there," Lucy said.

"I can borrow a cellular phone," Lucas told her. "I was planning to anyway. And the same friend can lend me a small tape recorder and microphone that I can tape to my chest. If we witness Shi confessing or even threatening us, then a recording of what we heard is admissible evidence." He leaned back in the white plastic chair. "I'm getting a good feeling about this," he said. "I think things are going to click into place."

"I sure hope they do," Slocum responded. "I'm really looking forward to having this whole thing finally settled one way or the other. I've got a life somewhere that needs living." He gazed off through the window for a moment. "Can you imagine all the excuses I'll be able to pick from when I'm back at school. 'Sorry, Professor Mooney, I was being held captive in a rec room until I revealed a spiritual secret.' Or 'I would've been here sooner but I was busy dodging the police on a murder rap.'" He shook his head wistfully. "How soon can we get this thing over with?"

"How about tonight?" Lucas answered. "Is that soon enough?"

Slocum grinned. "What do you think, Luce?"

"Sounds good to me, but what's with this 'Loose' thing?"

"Luce for Lucy. Get used to it."

"Okie-dokie Slokie."

"I think I'll leave you two alone," Lucas announced. "I've got a lot to do to get ready for tonight." He pushed back his chair and stood.

"What do we need to do?" Lucy asked.

"Hang out, stay out of sight, argue over cute nicknames — whatever you like. Let's meet in the lighthouse parking lot at nine. That should give us plenty of time to run through everything."

"Wait a minute. Aren't you going to go over the plan now?" Slocum protested.

Lucas shook his head. "There isn't any specific plan at this point. I need to do reconnaissance out at the meeting site, see just what equipment's available to us — things like that. Don't worry. I'll have it all worked out by tonight."

"What do we need to bring?" Lucy asked.

"Warm clothes. Maybe a thermos of coffee if you drink it. That's all I can think of," Lucas replied.

"All right. See you at nine," Lucy told him as he strode to the door.

"Good luck," Slocum called.

"I don't believe in luck," Lucas told him, halting and turning to explain. "Everything will turn out the way it needs to. It always does."

"Do you think it needs us to die?" Lucy asked, her voice unsteady.

"We'll find out," Lucas answered evenly, and then he was gone.

Twenty-Two

Slocum convinced Lucy to drive into town for groceries at ten forty-five. He had to feign a craving for Dr. Pepper to motivate her since there was already a considerable array of items in her refrigerator. Greg called at eleven.

"So fill me in," he requested.

"I'm not sure how much time we've got," Slocum said, "so I'm going to rush through everything new. Then we need to plan — you'll see why when I tell you what's up. If there's time, then I'll fill you in more thoroughly. Okay?"

"Sure. Go ahead."

So Slocum crammed the last twelve hours into fifteen minutes. When he was finished, he grew aware of something nibbling at the veil in his psyche that separated his conscious from his unconscious. In the midst of his account, a tidbit had triggered a 'knowing' that wasn't quite ready to emerge. He told Greg to hang on a minute and tried to at least glean a sense of what sort of thing it might be.

It was important; that much he knew intuitively. And then he realized that there had been a clue in his story — a key element — that definitively answered the most important question: who was the bad guy? For the life of him, though, he didn't know what the hell it was.

He explained this to Greg and asked him if any particular thing had jumped out at him.

"No, not really. Overall, it struck me that this Chinese guy is probably the murderer, but it wasn't any one thing that convinced me. And it could be Lucas — or even Lucy."

"Oh well. Let's talk about how to deal with this meeting tonight. Any ideas?"

"Do you think we need an even better plan than the cue commando deal?"

"Yes."

"Hmm. I'll just put my thinking cap on."

"You do that."

They hashed it out for over a half hour, occasionally checking with Flinch about various matters. Eventually, everyone was satisfied that their asses were covered as well as possible, given all the givens. Actually, Flinch's judgment was that they'd developed a "fucking brilliant plan." Greg pronounced it "adequate for our needs," because it had mostly been Slocum's idea. And Slocum himself was too preoccupied with his futile lost tidbit retrieval process to pay much attention. Whenever his mind wasn't otherwise occupied, he inventoried his memory and played with whatever he uncovered.

There was enough time left over for Greg to ask questions for a while before Lucy got back. He exhausted all his legitimate concerns fairly quickly, and resorted to silly questions that Slocum wasn't in the mood for. He hung up on his friend and wished he'd done it sooner; Greg could be incredibly self-indulgent.

Lucy arrived soon after, two grocery bags under her arms. Karma trooped in with her; apparently the front porch wasn't as absorbing as usual.

"I had to go to two places to get you that damned soda," she told Slocum, dumping the bags unceremoniously on the kitchen table. Karma sprawled in front of the bathroom door.

"Thanks. I appreciate it. That's what youngin's in Texas were raised on in the old days, you know."

"Yeah?"

"Well just until they were twelve or thirteen and they switched to Pearl or Lone Star beer, of course."

"Of course."

Both of them began to empty the bags' contents on the table.

"I bought more of everything than we could possibly use right now," Lucy confessed. "It was kind of a way of reassuring myself that we'll be alive tomorrow."

"That makes sense."

Lucy cocked her head. "What's that noise?" she asked.

Slocum moved to the window. "Oh shit. It's those two detectives that arrested me. They must've tagged you in town. Is there a back door? What am I talking about? I know there isn't."

"Hide under the bed," Lucy instructed. "Quick! I'll pull the comforter down."

Slocum scrambled onto the floor and rolled under her bed. It was a tight squeeze. Karma watched him with vague interest.

"Watch out for the quiet one," Slocum warned in a stage whisper. "They're both real sharp."

"Shh. I'll be fine. I'm a great actress — remember?" She finished positioning the bed clothes and moved back to the table.

A moment later, the police knocked on the door. Slocum couldn't see anything but he could hear fairly well. It was dusty under the bed and smelled like old socks. He hoped he didn't have to hide for too long.

"Hello?" Lucy greeted them, the epitome of innocence.

"Hello, ma'am," Perry said. "We're police officers and I'm afraid we need to ask you a few questions."

"Can I see some I.D.?"

"Of course."

Things were quiet, presumably while Lucy studied their badges.

"Well, come on in. You can sit at the table if you like. I'm just putting away my groceries."

There was the sound of chairs scraping and plastic packages being moved.

Sergeant Morino spoke up next. "Boy, I guess you really like Dr. Pepper a lot, huh?" His voice was so cultured it was hard to believe he was a cop, let alone bore a resemblance to a labrador retriever.

"It's my boyfriend. He's crazy about the stuff."

Not a trace of nervousness or any other false note betrayed her voice.

"It was originally a Texas product, wasn't it?" Morino asked.

He was a sly bastard, Slocum conceded — always coming in the side door.

"Gee, I don't know," Lucy answered casually. "Maybe so. Karma! Lie down!" she called. "You *can't* go get on the bed. Don't even think about it."

Slocum held his breath and hoped his furry buddy would lose interest in him.

"That's a handsome animal. What kind of dog is it?" Perry asked.

"The kind that always wants to lie on something soft. Look at her — heading over to the bed again. Karma! I'm just going to put you out." Lucy's steps hurried over to where Slocum was sequestered. Judging by the sound, she must've caught Karma with only inches to spare.

"Now out you go."

Once she'd returned to her seat, Perry spoke. "Looks like you've had some company," he said.

"You mean the dishes? Well, my boyfriend was over last night and we had breakfast together. But let's get on with this, all right? What do you need to talk to me about?"

"Him," Perry replied. "Have you ever seen this man?"

"That's Slocum Happler," Lucy answered.

"So you know him."

"Sure. We had dinner together the other night. Has something happened to him?"

There was a pause and Slocum pictured the detective holding up a hand.

"Bear with me," he requested.

"Sure. Whatever."

"How'd you meet him?" Perry asked.

"Earlier that same day we bumped into each other at the Long Marine Lab," Lucy answered.

"Slocum was under the impression that you worked there," Perry told her.

"Oh no. I was just visiting — I wanted to see the dolphins."

"Can you think of any reason for him to come to that conclusion?"

"That I worked there? Not really. He was kind of nervous, though. I think the way I looked intimidated him."

"Why'd you go out with him if you have a boyfriend?" Morino asked.

"It wasn't a date kind of thing. Is that what he told you? It's just that he seemed like a nice guy and I don't know too many people around here."

"New to the area, are you?" Morino asked.

"Uh huh. Are you guys ever going to tell me what this is all about?"

"Please," Perry implored politely. "Just a few more questions."

"And then you'll fill me in?"

"I promise."

"Well, okay then."

"Would you tell us your full name please?" Perry asked.

"You guys don't even know my name? Oh this is too much."

Slocum heard her move over to her purse and rummage inside it.

"Here you go. Vanessa Woods. That's me."

"Thank you," Perry replied.

"You don't read the newspaper, do you?" Morino asked.

"Nope. And as you can see, I don't have a radio or a TV either," Lucy told him. "So you guys are going to be the ones to tell me about Slocum. And I mean now. I've been patient."

"Miss Woods," Perry began. "Slocum Happler is wanted for questioning in a murder investigation."

"Slocum? No way. You've got the wrong guy," she protested.

"Perhaps. Have you seen or heard from him since your dinner with him?"

"No. He doesn't even have my phone number."

"And this was four nights ago you saw him?" Morino asked.

"No. Three. We ate at the Zapoteca."

"Do you know anyone named Lucas?" Perry asked.

"No. Should I?"

"Did you see anyone you know at the restaurant?"

"Sure. My friend Marcus. He's a big guy with a beard."

Her exasperated tone seemed just perfect to Slocum. Anyone would be tired of all these questions by now.

The chairs scraped again and Slocum heard footsteps.

"Well, thank you for your time," Perry told her.

"No problem."

"We can be back tomorrow with a warrant," Morino suddenly growled, his tone completely different than it had been in the rest of the interview. He was trying to sound mean.

"Whatever for?"

"You'd be the best judge of that, ma'am."

"You think I'm hiding your suspect in my closet? Is that it? I hardly know the guy, for Chrissakes."

"We'll keep that in mind, ma'am," Perry replied. "Good day."

"Bye."

Various noises signalled their departure but Slocum didn't budge until Lucy pulled up the comforter.

"How'd I do?" Lucy asked.

"You're a marvel." Slocum climbed out and gave her a hug. "You've got nerves of steel."

"Talent is what I've got, Sloke. Gobs of it."

"Hey, I'm not arguing. But those guys must know more than they're letting on or they wouldn't have recognized you and followed you here. Just don't get cocky, babe."

"Moi? Never." She kissed him hard and he shut up.

Twenty-Three

Slocum and Lucy passed the eight hours before meeting Lucas in a variety of ways. They ate, walked the dog, read, made love, napped, and swapped life stories. The latter activity, pursued while lying naked in bed, revealed an uncanny lack of common experiences or circumstances. Lucy grew up in an apartment, Slocum in an old farm house. Lucy was an only child, Slocum had two brothers and a sister. Lucy loved jazz and hated classical music; Slocum's preferences were just the reverse.

It got so that if Lucy said something such as "I love Thai food," she'd just go ahead and add, "and of course you don't."

Slocum would nod and try one back at her. "I had a zillion cavities as a kid, so naturally you've always had perfect teeth, right?"

He sat up against a pillow; Lucy lay on her back, looking up at the ceiling. A yellow sheet covered her legs and part of the furry patch of strawberry blond pubic hair that trailed off in a line of fuzz going up to her navel.

"Naturally," she replied. "Except once I spent a whole summer eating candy at girl scout camp so I got one cavity."

"I never went away to camp," Slocum told her, glancing at her face. She seemed to have fewer freckles than she used to.

"Of course not. And I'll bet you weren't a boy scout either."

"No. My mom said they were fascists."

And so on.

Later, while lying with their legs entwined and Lucy's breast pressed against his arm, Slocum tried to make sense out of the phenomenon.

"Maybe the old 'opposites attract' maxim has some legitimate basis. I mean there has to be something unusual going on to generate this much sexual energy."

"Maybe," Lucy replied distractedly. She seemed more interested in arranging herself so that her nipple poked directly into Slocum's armpit.

"But then why do we like each other?" Slocum asked.

"What do you mean?" Lucy was listening now.

"Well, most couples get together because they have a lot in common, right?"

Lucy rolled away from him and sat up against the wall, pulling the sheet up around her waist. She focused intently on his face as she responded heatedly. "Whoa. Hold it, fella. Who said anything about a couple here? I like you and fate has sort of thrown us into each other's arms, but that's it. We're *not* a couple. I'll admit the sex is fantastic, but when this is all over, I'm heading back down to L.A. and getting on with my career. I thought you understood that."

"Hey, I'm not proposing marriage. Calm down," Slocum told her, motioning with palms-down hands.

"I just want to be real clear about this," Lucy replied. "I've been accused of mishandling this kind of situation in the past."

"It's happened before?"

"No, Slocum. I'm a virgin." Lucy's face was contorted with sarcasm; it was ugly.

"I mean you've gotten involved with people before when you knew it was just a temporary thing?" Slocum asked.

"We're *not* involved. Aren't you listening to me?"

"Well, whatever we are. We're something. I'm just double-checking that this is an experience you've had before."

"Right. It is." She folded her arms across her breasts.

"Well, it's new to me." He sat up too and faced her across the width of the double bed. He felt a little exposed by his nudity, but he made a conscious decision not to cover up.

"Bullshit," she spat.

"I mean it. I've always been in love with someone before I got physical. I guess it's just another way we're different."

"I hate that phrase 'got physical' " She mimicked him harshly as she said it. "Just say 'fucked', okay? Just say what you really mean for once. Anyway, you're just talking about typical male self-delusion," Lucy accused. "First you convince yourself that it's some big romantic fantasy, then you go ahead and get laid, which was what you wanted in the first place."

"Let me take a wild guess here, Lucy. You've been hurt by men, right?"

"Try and find a woman who hasn't — that's beside the point."

Slocum was able to find that place within himself that didn't take things personally. He reached over and placed his hand over hers. "I'm not trying to get something from you or make you do anything. Honestly. I'm sorry I made it sound like that. I really am."

She looked up at him, reserving judgment on his sincerity.

"I know we're not a serious couple," he continued. "I know it's circumstances that have pushed us at each other, and I know you'll go back to your career. I'm not trying to change the facts. I was just interested in how things work between us." Slocum held her hand now in both of his and waited for her response.

"Oh." Her posture softened and the sheet slid down her torso. "Well I'm sorry if I overreacted. And I *will* miss you when I go."

"I'll miss you two," he said, staring overtly at her exposed breasts to evince the pun.

Trying not to smile, Lucy snatched her hand away and slapped him gently. "That's awful."

"It's the truth. And there are other parts I'll miss just as much."

"Yeah? Like what?"

"Here." He showed her. "And here." He demonstrated just what he'd miss doing.

"Mmm," she murmured. "You've got a point there."

"No, my point's over here." He guided her hand to him.

"Good point."

"Thank-you. Want to make me pointless?"

"Sure." So she did.

* * *

At eight forty p.m., Lucy drove down the rugged dirt road beside her cabin, and Slocum once again weathered the experience on the floorboards of a cheap car. His bruised hip and shoulder were very unhappy with the seating arrangements. Instead of a paper bag over his head, though, this time he was covered by a light cotton blanket, which was a substantial improvement. Karma sat up in front in the passenger seat; she rode proud and free — like some people used to, Slocum thought. Then his mind shifted to the memory of the policemen's visit.

"Remember to keep an eye out for anyone following you," Slocum said from under his covering.

"I can't hear you," Lucy replied.

He moved aside the corner of the blanket nearest his mouth and repeated himself.

"I will," she assured him.

"How's Karma doing?"

"She's having a great time. I've got her strapped in with the safety belt. But I'm still not sure we should've brought her."

"We need all the help we can get. Anyway, she really didn't want to stay there by herself." The truth was that Slocum had a vague notion that he might need the dog's discriminatory powers before the night was through. If she bit Feng Shi, or wagged her tail three times when she met him, for instance, her input could be very useful. Also, Slocum figured that Lucas wouldn't want her there. By bringing Karma, he'd immediately force a confrontation, which could help balance the skewed power between himself and Lucas.

For some reason, he found that he didn't want to go into all that with Lucy. It wasn't exactly that he didn't trust her, it was more like he didn't see the point of taking unnecessary risks.

"You know," Lucy began, as she turned onto the paved country road that led to Santa Cruz proper, "I'm surprised that we haven't heard from Greg."

"Oh, I'm sure he's out there working on my behalf," Slocum responded. "He's a good friend."

"I think he's a crack-up too," she added. "I've never met anybody so funny."

"Maybe he and I'll come visit you down south sometime."

"Sounds good. By the way, we're not being followed unless they're invisible."

"I'm going back under my blanket then."

"Right. See ya. Oh, Slocum — one more thing. Are you nervous about tonight?"

"Scared out of my mind, actually."

"Me too."

Twenty-Four

They encountered a dense fog as Lucy guided the car onto West Cliff Drive and gently accelerated towards the lighthouse. If anything, it became even thicker as they neared the parking lot beside the local landmark. This wasn't unusual, but as Slocum crawled up onto the back seat, he was surprised simply because he had pictured the scene dozens of times that day without fog. In fact, he'd simply retrieved his last image of the lighthouse — the morning he'd met Saddhu Ramba — and darkened it for imagination's sake. He felt an irrational stab of disappointment that reality hadn't cooperated with his mind's eye.

Lucas' truck was parked in a corner of the lot, but he was nowhere in sight. Several street lights lit the fringes of the area with an orange glow, but the fog restrained the illumination from penetrating the heart of the scene. The lighthouse itself squandered its anemic beam out over the dark waters. Lucas, then, could simply have settled in sufficiently distant from the light sources. Another possibility, Slocum reasoned, was that he was lurking behind the old brick building.

Once released from the car, Karma evaluated the situation and trotted directly to the door of the surfing museum in the lighthouse. Then she stood alertly in front of it as if she were reading some coded message in the wood grain, or perhaps seeing through the door to the colorful displays inside.

Slocum filled his lungs with fresh air as he climbed out of the small car. Strong doses of seaweed and fish odor rushed into his chest and he coughed. The water vapor in the air transported the nearby sea aromas with little loss of potency. For a moment, Slocum was severely nauseated as well, and he recalled the other morning when spoiled yogurt had triggered a similar response.

"Are you okay?" Lucy asked, stepping around the rear of the car to hand him a gray oversized wool sweater.

Slocum nodded; the discomfort had come and gone quickly. He slipped the sweater on and patted his curly black hair into place.

"What's that weird sound?" Lucy asked after she'd followed suit, pulling her crystal pendant out over her dark green sweater.

Slocum hadn't heard anything, but as soon as he paid attention, the cacophony was almost overwhelming, and he couldn't believe he'd missed it.

"It's the sea lions on seal rock," he told her, motioning with a thumb. "They're really going nuts tonight."

It sounded as though dogs from other planets were holding a contest to see who could produce the most unearthly bark or howl.

"What do you think Karma's doing?" Lucy asked, peering through the gloom.

"Beats me. Maybe she was a surfer in a former life."

"That doesn't make sense."

"Reincarnation? I thought Zen people believed in that."

"No, I mean going from a surfer to this," she responded, gesturing with an outstretched arm at the dog. "She must've been at least a pope last time."

"That's a nice thought."

The gash on Slocum's forehead throbbed; it was the one injury that wasn't healing properly.

"Come on, let's go," Lucy suggested, holding out her hand for Slocum to take.

He clasped it and together they trudged toward the lighthouse, looking like dental patients en route from their teeth cleaning to the main event with the nasty dentist himself.

The sea lions were suddenly quiet and the silence, by contrast, seemed to be the deepest hush Slocum had ever experienced.

In the dim light, the building assumed a very different mien than it had displayed during the day. The two-story tower rose over the rectangular brick building it adjoined, creating a shape that was neither fish nor fowl. Too stubby and stunted to truly evoke the image of a lighthouse, it was also too bizarre an architectural feature to suggest a home, office, or any other mundane structure. In the sunlight, it was cute. At ten p.m., in the fog, it was a disturbing hybrid, seemingly beyond rational understanding. Slocum could tell himself that it was a memorial or a toy lighthouse, but those were just concepts. The visual reality insisted on its due, engendering a foreboding that he couldn't banish.

Even details such as the catwalk around the top portion of the lighthouse tower seemed to augment Slocum's uneasiness. He had no idea why. The decorative black wrought iron fencing and the potted flowers — these he could comprehend. They were there to entice him, to lure him to his doom. But what could a catwalk do to him?

As Slocum and Lucy neared the panelled door of the lighthouse, it swung open from the inside. Karma growled.

"Why did you bring the dog?" Lucas hissed from just inside the threshold.

"She wanted to come," Slocum replied neutrally.

"It's an additional variable," Lucas told him impatiently. His dispassionate mask was slipping badly. "Put her in the car," he ordered.

"No," Slocum replied, stepping up next to Karma and scratching her ear.

"No?"

"You heard me. The dog stays," Slocum replied forcefully. "Or we all go."

"Feeling your oats, eh? Well you'd better come on in here, I guess. And bring the dog. But for God's sake, keep her quiet."

"Isn't this breaking and entering?" Lucy asked as she moved forward with Karma by her side.

"Just trespassing," Lucas responded, stepping to one side of the doorway. "You're walking through an open door, aren't you?"

"Did you?" Slocum asked, crossing the threshold behind Lucy.

Lucas didn't answer as he closed the door behind them.

A kerosene lantern sat in the middle of the concrete floor, its wick trimmed short. Several other objects lay nearby — Lucas' shotgun, a red day-pack, and a cellular phone. Displays of surfboards, clothing, posters, and photographs hung on the brick interior walls. Dimly lit from the lantern below, the museum could just as well have been dedicated to early rocketry as surfing.

Lucas was wearing a brown jump suit with an aviation company's name and logo embroidered in yellow across the chest. Granger Air Freight's logo was a capital 'G' holding a suitcase shaped like a bird. Or maybe it was a bird shaped like a suitcase. Either way it seemed to Slocum to be an odd choice of attire.

"What's with the outfit?" he asked.

"I need to do laundry," Lucas replied, smiling his peculiar smile.

Karma padded across the floor and lay down on an antique wooden surfboard.

Lucas moved further into the room and stood in front of Slocum and Lucy. Illuminated from below, his eyes were dark holes above his hirsute cheeks. It was an eerie effect that didn't inspire trust.

"Lucy," he began, "you'll be in here with the telephone. And the dog," he added, glaring at Slocum. "I've set the redial function for 911, and I phoned in an anonymous tip to the police so they'll be ready to act on a call about the murders this evening."

"When do I call?" Lucy asked.

"When I signal you," Lucas answered. "I'll be about thirty feet away from the lighthouse towards the water."

"On the grass?"

"Precisely. With the door cracked open you should have no problem seeing me raise my right arm."

"That's the signal?"

"Right. Just like a kindergartner asking permission to go to the bathroom."

This comparison struck Slocum as being wildly inappropriate. How could such an image coalesce in anyone's brain in this context? He spoke up so he wouldn't have to think about it anymore.

"What about me? I get the shotgun, right?"

"Yes. It's loaded with birdshot, but I doubt you'll need to do anything but brandish it if things go wrong."

"Brandish it?"

"Wave it around. Show it. An ounce of prevention is worth a pound of cure."

"Did you learn that one in India?" Lucy asked sweetly.

Lucas ignored her. "You'll be outside, Slocum," he instructed. "Lying down by the fence near the edge of the cliff. That will place you a little farther away than Lucy, but the street lights in the background should render my arm motions quite clear. If I raise my left arm, that's your cue to come forward with the gun."

"Right. Now what's the rest of the plan?"

"That's about it," Lucas replied, crossing his arms.

"Well, what are you going to do?" Lucy asked.

"Meet with Feng Shi. Try to entice him into revealing enough to incriminate himself."

"What's to stop him from just killing you?" Slocum asked.

"He likes to talk. And I know some things he wants to know."

"Are you willing to stake your life on that?"

"Yes."

Lucy spoke next. "Didn't you say something about our hearing the conversation too so we could be witnesses?"

"Yes. Thanks for reminding me, Lucy," he said, but he actually seemed annoyed at her. He reached down and extracted some equipment from the red backpack. "Each of you gets a headset and a receiver." The receivers were no bigger than cigarette packs; the headset consisted of two lightweight foam pads on a vinyl-covered metal clip. "I've got a recorder and transmitter strapped to me so you two will hear everything I hear."

Lucas showed Slocum and Lucy how to operate the electronic gear, which was fairly simple.

"I feel like a refugee from a TV cop show with all this," Lucy said.

"Me too," Slocum agreed. "This is a high-tech operation, Lucas."

"You've got to change with the times," the older man responded. "Life is change. You change or you die."

Slocum couldn't think of anything to say in response to that; Lucy was silent as well.

"We'd better assume our positions," Lucas told them. "Follow me, Slocum."

"Wait a minute. Aren't you going to show me how the gun works?"

"I thought you said you were familiar with shotguns." Once again, Lucas seemed irritated — even cranky.

"Not this one. Where's the safety, for example?"

Lucas showed him impatiently and then thrust the gun at him. "Come on," he ordered.

Slocum made a show out of taking his time hugging Lucy and whispering "good luck" in her ear. Then he followed Lucas out into the fog, cradling the shotgun across his chest.

The fence by the clifftop was constructed of rounded metal posts and struts, which curved inward at the top. About three feet tall, the fence was designed to keep tourists from being swept out to sea by freakish waves. It happened a few times a year anyway, since visitors tended to climb over the barrier to line up more dramatic camera angles.

Slocum's observation post was a shallow depression in the damp earth beside the fence. He couldn't tell whether Lucas had scooped it out himself or merely discovered it. After checking the gun, Slocum lay prone and waited, which in this instance entailed doubting all the plans and morosely dwelling on everything that could go wrong. He tried to discipline his mind and his abject failure to do so reminded him of Baba's likening the ego to a crazy monkey. This, in turn, led him to Saddhu's advice about listening to the inner teacher that lived in his heart.

It was easy figuring out which of his inner counselors lived in his testicles, for example, but narrowing the field down to the heart seemed impossible. There was a part of his mind, Slocum knew, that was a simulacrum of his heart — a reductionist representation of what his truest part meant in purely mental terms. He'd been conned by this voice more times than he'd care to remember. And he knew that simply swapping all that for the realm of raw emotions wasn't what Saddhu meant either. There was a profound distinction between emotions and heart, typified by love with a lower case 'l' and Love with a capital 'L'. But knowing such things — being able to label what *wasn't* his inner teacher — was meager help in intuiting what the hell to do in a given situation.

Slocum tried to understand his current circumstances in terms of which inner voices had been guiding him. It seemed to him that tracing things back might yield a fresh perspective that could help him survive the impending confrontation. Unfortunately, the endeavor proved to be far too ambitious — he was completely unsuccessful.

The effort did help pass the time, though, and take his mind off his physical discomfort. It was cold out on the spit of land that jutted into the chilly waters. The fog was an ally of the cold, employing its vapors to penetrate Slocum's clothes and thoroughly chill him. What he needed was some kind of waterproof shell over Lucy's bulky sweater. And a squad of marines would help too. Instead, he had the shivers, Greg, and Flinch.

Twenty-Five

Eventually, an ugly white motor scooter pulled into the lighthouse parking lot. The part of the scooter that sat over the rear wheel bulged out grotesquely on the sides as if it were about to burst open. Through the fog, Slocum could discern that the lone rider, clad in black leather, was a medium-sized male.

The man parked, dismounted, and strode forward. Surely this was not the elderly Chinese man they were awaiting. Would Lucas be able to get rid of whoever it was?

The man made a beeline for the lighthouse, Lucas called from where he stood on the lawn.

"Shi! I'm over here. Namaste."

It *was* Feng Shi; Slocum's expectations were once again thoroughly defied.

As the man veered to approach the bearded guru, Slocum heard a 'click' and then the voices of Shi and Lucas were clear through the headset.

"Marcus. You are looking well."

"Thank you," Lucas/Marcus responded.

"Now it is only us two," Shi said.

The man's voice was very odd. Not only did he have a complicated accent--only vaguely Chinese--but his intonation and rhythm were practically arbitrary. It was as if all the words were being spun around in his head like the numbered bails in a church bingo game, and then when it was time to say the next one, it would pop out whichever way it happened to be turned. Slocum had never heard anything like it.

"How does it feel," Lucas asked, "to have murdered two of the most advanced souls on the planet?"

Slocum could see that Lucas was holding his right hand up by his shoulder, wriggling mudras at his nemesis.

"It feels good. But not as good as taking care of you will feel," Shi replied, flashing mudras back at him. His style was more expansive, replete with arm and head movements.

It looked pretty silly to Slocum, but for all he knew they could actually be marshalling titanic primal forces or screwing around with the fabric of the universe somehow. He certainly didn't consider himself competent to judge things like that.

"Why did you wait and target me last?" Lucas asked.

"You were useful. You and your young friends."

Feng Shi's weird speech pattern was even worse now. And something about it bothered Slocum more than it should've.

"What do you plan for me?" Lucas asked. "More needles? A chop to the adam's apple?"

"Perhaps. We shall see."

Slocum gripped the shotgun tighter, thumbed back the safety, and curled his right index finger on the trigger. He just hoped he'd be in time if he needed to use it.

"Tell me why," Lucas said. "Why all the killing?"

"You know why. I am Brahmachari's heir."

Both men were still furiously trading mudras.

"His Judas, you mean. It was written that the purest reflection of our Master's love would be the next Guru of Gurus."

"We find that the meaning of this expression is very similar to that...."

Slocum was jolted and stopped listening. This last phrase, smoothly spoken without Feng Shi's characteristic halting inflection, triggered things in him. In fact, Slocum was so stunned that his bent index finger flexed involuntarily. The shotgun's response — a metallic thump — confirmed the revelation that had clicked into place inside him. He'd already had all the clues filed away somewhere, but the murderer's carelessness catalyzed a synthesis — now he knew.

The question was: how much would knowing help? He was holding a useless weapon and the plan he'd concocted with Greg and Flinch might or might not work now. He needed to think things through, armed with his new knowledge, and determine just what to do. Fortunately, as he began analyzing the elements of his predicament, he discovered that he could focus clearly and concentrate well. It was the first time he'd truly felt like himself in days.

A few minutes later, as Feng Shi directly confessed his guilt in stilted vocabulary over the headphones, Lucas raised both his arms. Slocum scrambled to his feet and moved forward through the fog, the shotgun aimed at the Chinese man, who awaited him calmly. Slocum stripped off the headset and halted about six feet away.

"Good," Lucas told him. "Don't get too close. Shi is capable of substantial physical mayhem."

Feng Shi was a very impressive man. His face betrayed his age, yet there was a child's vitality in his dark eyes. The light wasn't good enough for a thorough appraisal of him, but Slocum sensed both his substantiality and his rock-solid peace of mind. There was a lot to the man and none of it was off-center.

"Slocum Happler, I assume?" Shi asked. His inflection was perfectly normal.

"That's right. Hi."

"It seems that Marcus has corrupted you, after all."

Before Slocum could reply, Lucy called from the museum doorway. "I can't get the phone to work!"

"Come on out," Lucas shouted. "I'll see what I can do."

Lucy walked out, leaving the door ajar behind her. "I'm sure I'm pressing the right button," she said as she approached the others with the telephone.

"I'm sure you are too," Lucas agreed, reaching down to his ankle and then straightening up with a semi-automatic pistol in his hand. "Stand next to the Chinaman, sweetheart."

In shock, her eyes wide and vacant, Lucy stumbled to the side of the old man.

Slocum realized that he'd made a mistake covering Feng Shi with the impotent shotgun. All he'd done was prevent the martial arts expert from acting on everyone's behalf when Lucas went for his gun.

He pivoted and trained the gun on Lucas, who kept his handgun aimed at Feng Shi.

"Drop the gun," Slocum told him.

"The shotgun is loaded with dud shells," Lucas replied, grinning.

"Not anymore." Slocum reached into his pants pocket and tossed Lucas' green plastic shells onto the lawn by the bearded man's feet. "I decided to use my own ammo," he elaborated.

"You're bluffing," Lucas replied, his expression reverting to neutral.

"So how'd I know to take out your shells, then?"

"Perhaps when I told you you'd only need to brandish it, you decided to take me literally. Perhaps you're a pacifist. I don't know. But you haven't got the brains to have figured this out. That much I know." Lucas' tone was contemptuous and Slocum felt his face flush.

"Try me," he barked aggressively.

"How'd I kill Saddhu if I was talking to Lucy at the time?"

"She's holding the answer in her hands," Slocum replied, "The cellular phone. You killed him *while* you were talking to her. You probably played a recording for the background noise."

Lucy gaped at Lucas. "God, you're a cold-blooded bastard," she told him, "You were calm as you could be."

Lucas acknowledged her with a nod and then spoke again to Slocum.

"How about the conversation here tonight? Don't you believe your ears, Slocum?"

"You put together a tape and you sent it out to us while the real conversation was going on."

"Put together a tape? Whatever do you mean?"

"Don't play with us," Feng Shi answered. "We're not idiots."

"Speak for yourself, Shi. I've had this boy jumping through hoops for days."

"You're not that clever, Lucas," Slocum retorted. "It's all just a bunch of electronic mumbo-jumbo. You got hold of tapes of Feng Shi giving lectures, then you pilfered it in bits and pieces so he'd seem to be giving you and Lucy orders over the phone. Tonight's just more of the same tired stunt. I don't have to be smart to figure you out, old man."

Slocum's cockiness was partly a by-product of his bruised ego and partly calculated. It seemed to him that this was the way a man with a loaded shotgun would act — as if his adversary's feelings and reactions no longer mattered.

"So how'd you guess all this?" Lucas asked.

"Guess? I didn't guess, you arrogant son of a bitch."

"Whatever." Lucas waved away Slocum's reaction with his free hand. "What gave me away?"

If he'd stopped here, Slocum's play might've worked, but, new to the intrigue business and sufficiently immature to be susceptible to manipulation, he couldn't leave well enough alone.

"It was that phrase, 'We find the meaning of this experience is very similar....'"

Feng Shi spoke up again. "Salt Lake City, 1986," he said.

"Carmel, 1989," Lucas corrected.

"Anyway," Slocum continued, his pride interfering with his common sense, "you played that in your motel room and then again tonight. That's really sloppy, old man."

Lucas' eyes gleamed and his lips pulled back. "I think I understand," he responded. "You figured all this out about ten minutes ago and you emptied the gun in a futile effort to bluff me.

"No, no," Slocum protested. "I knew it when I heard the tape at the motel. Access to Feng Shi's voice was the missing link. I know how sophisticated answering machines and electronic phones can be. My dad's got one that can dial and send messages on its own."

"Your father works in a warehouse," Lucas reminded him.

"So? He could still have a fancy phone."

"He doesn't. You're not a very good liar, Slocum."

"Okay, fine," he replied, tossing the shotgun down onto the dewy lawn. "I've got a plan 'B.' Actually a plan 'C' too, but I don't think we'll need that."

"Don't ever play poker," Lucas told him. "Hey Shi," he added, "remember those all-night games in Hyderabad?"

"Certainly." The man's tone of voice was still completely centered. "The winner was always one of us, although I think I might have won a few more times than you."

"Tonight should square us," Lucas answered.

"Flinch!" Slocum called.

Lucas gazed at him blankly.

"At your service," the coarse voice replied from behind Lucas.

As the guru whirled, Flinch pumped a shell into his shotgun. "Don't try it," the homeless man warned. "I ain't killed nobody lately but I'm pretty good at it."

He was wearing his army combat fatigues and he stood confidently, showing his ruined teeth.

"I'd like to point something out," Lucas told him. "The others are standing directly behind me."

He whirled again and covered the threesome with his pistol. "Don't move," he counseled them. Calling loudly to Flinch behind him, Lucas continued. "If you shoot and miss, you'll hit a civilian. And even if you hit me, at this range the chances are some of it will go through and hit them too. I'll bet you've got at least buckshot in there — am I right?"

Flinch didn't answer since he was stealthily moving forward and to the side to get the drop on Lucas. He stumbled momentarily on a sprinkler head, though.

Lucas turned and raised the pistol to fire as Flinch regained his balance and aimed the shotgun.

Then a dark form flashed into view and launched itself at Lucas. Karma's arrival was virtually simultaneous with the blasts of both guns and it was impossible to tell what had happened.

Feng Shi was a blur, pulling Lucy over to Slocum. "Follow me," he told them, sprinting away from the lights towards the ocean.

The shotgun fired again as Slocum and Lucy ran after the amazingly fast Chinese man. As they reached the fence near where Slocum had lain hidden, Shi was vaulting over it.

"This way," he whispered.

Slocum and Lucy clambered over the metal rail and joined him on the wet, rocky clifftop. The threesome flattened themselves and surveyed the area they'd just departed through the fence struts. There was nothing to see.

Slocum lay in the middle, flanked by Lucy on his right and Feng Shi on his left. Already the dampness was seeping through his clothes.

"What happened?" Slocum asked Shi.

"I believe the dog and I took the brunt of the shotgun pellets. I think your military friend was hit by Marcus' pistol shot too. I don't know how seriously. We should be safe here for a while — the light favors us."

Just then Flinch's voice boomed across the grass. "I'm back in my hole guys. And that hairy cocksucker is either in the lighthouse or behind it. I don't know where the dog is." He paused for air, then continued shouting. "I took a slug in the leg, but the asshole's not going anywhere 'cuz I got a line on the parking lot side of things. Don't answer me and give away your positions. And Greg!" He raised his raspy voice even more. "Stay where you are!"

"What did he mean 'back in his hole?'" Lucy whispered.

"That's where he's been hiding," Slocum told her. "He dug a hole and pulled sod over himself."

"Why didn't you tell me? And what's Greg doing?"

"Shh," Feng Shi cautioned. "We must plan."

"How bad are you hit?" Slocum asked.

"One shoulder is no longer functional," he reported calmly. "And I'll be weak with blood loss soon."

"Damn. I was thinking that one way out was into the water, but you can't go that route, can you?"

"No. And it's too dangerous anyway. Fortunately I don't need both shoulders to deal with Marcus if he's out in the open. And if he's in the lighthouse, your friend has him trapped and one of you can go for the police."

"The shots may bring them anyway," Slocum pointed out.

"That's true," Shi agreed in an accented whisper.

"But how do we know which one it is — where Lucas is, I mean?"

"Lucas is Marcus?"

"Yes."

"I will find out," Shi answered. "If he's behind the building, I'll deal with him."

"Is that really a good idea?" Lucy asked. "I mean you're wounded and all."

"I'm going now," he replied. "I think it would be best if you two stayed here."

"Right," Slocum replied.

"What if you don't come back?" Lucy asked.

"Pray," Shi suggested.

In one fluid motion, the Chinese man was up and over the fence. Silently, he moved to the left, circling behind the lighthouse.

"How old is that guy?" Lucy asked.

"Only about eighty or ninety. And he only got shot a little bit."

"Terrific."

"Relax. This is his milieu — he's a martial arts expert."

"Oh yeah. I forgot. So maybe we won't die."

Slocum put his wet, freezing arm around her. "Well, eventually. I don't think we can get out of that. But right now we'll just have to wait and see."

"Can you hold me?" Lucy asked.

He did.

Twenty-Six

It was relatively quiet for several minutes. Occasionally, a big wave slapped against the cliff high enough to startle Slocum and Lucy. And although the sea lions weren't still singing in ragged unison, the channel of water between Seal Rock and the cliff carried their conversations across as though they were right behind the duo. From the tone of their voices, the sea lions seemed to be complaining or arguing.

Suddenly the pistol fired three times and there was a sickening thud on the turf to the left. The flash of the gun betrayed Lucas' position; somehow he'd gotten up on the catwalk near the top of the light tower. The information wasn't much use, though, to Slocum and Lucy, and unfortunately the thud had sounded like the kind that precluded bouncing up and kicking ass. Feng Shi was probably out of commission.

For some reason, Flinch failed to return fire. It could be that from his angle he couldn't ascertain where the shots had been fired from, but another possibility was that he'd passed out. Slocum was rooting wholeheartedly for the former alternative. It was bad enough that he'd dragged the poor guy into all this. If Flinch was seriously hurt, it was going to be hard for Slocum to face himself in the bathroom mirror, assuming he ever got the chance.

He didn't know what to do. If Flinch was still conscious, then Lucas was pinned down in the lighthouse, unless he devised some way to rappel to the ground from the catwalk, which seemed unlikely to Slocum. In that scenario, then, time was on their side. Lucas would have to make a break for it before morning. And Slocum would definitely bet on a combat veteran armed with a shotgun in a foxhole against a man on the run with a pistol.

On the other hand, if Flinch had been hit bad enough, he'd be unconscious by now, and that dictated a totally different approach. One way to go would be for Slocum to try to hustle over and man the shotgun himself. Lucas' dispatching of Feng Shi, who was surely better at sneaking around than Slocum was, didn't bode well for that idea. Another possible scenario was that Lucas would realize that he was free to roam, and then just decide to split. Whatever his scheme had been, surely it was blown now. Maybe he'd cut his losses, make sure he missed the police, and jet off to Brazil or something. After all, he couldn't very well hunt for them all night. It was too risky.

"I think we should sit tight," Slocum ended up whispering to Lucy.

"If I tried to move, I'd pee my pants," Lucy replied. "Hell, I might anyway."

The door of the lighthouse swung open and Flinch failed to fire.

"Oh shit," Slocum exclaimed.

The tip of a surfboard poked out the doorway — still no response from Flinch. It looked like he wasn't going to be any help.

"Get back as far as you can," Slocum told Lucy. "We need to be as invisible as we can get."

As they wriggled on the slippery wet rock until their feet hung over the edge of the precipice behind them, the surfboard seemed to propel itself out onto the steps of the building. It was a long, hardwood board and Lucas hid behind it as he sidled towards the ocean. Halfway to where Slocum and Lucy lay, he threw down the board and jogged directly to the fence in front of them.

"I spotted you from the tower," he announced from five or six feet away. "One of you morons is wearing jewelry. You might as well stand up, by the way."

Slocum and Lucy climbed to their feet. She was fingering her pendant and mumbling apologies that no one heard.

Lucas gripped the pistol in his left hand; there was a considerable amount of blood dripping from his right. In his mechanic's coveralls, with his wild beard and loose long hair, he was a demonic figure out of some low-budget horror movie.

It suited him better than his earlier guises, Slocum realized. In a way, it was the first time he'd ever seen Lucas — the real Lucas.

"Are you going to kill us?" Lucy asked, her voice trembling.

"In a word — yes." Lucas' voice was supernaturally calm.

"Wait a minute. I want to ask something," Slocum said. He took Lucy's hand and squeezed it as he waited for a response.

"Ten seconds. I'll give you ten seconds," Lucas replied.

Karma was creeping on the lawn behind him, flattened like a reptile. One ear was gone and the raggedy hole was a gory mess. Her ribcage was even worse--you could see flesh hanging off her in shreds.

Slocum spoke quickly to cover any sound the dog might make. "Can we choose the way we die? What does it matter to you?" Karma was three or four feet away now. "How about we jump off the cliff? It'll save you a few bullets and we wouldn't have a chance. If the waves and the rocks don't get us, hypothermia will."

"No. I can't risk it. Sorry."

Lucy whimpered.

"Attack!" Slocum bellowed.

Lucas grinned inhumanly. "That's rather pathetic, Slo...."

And Karma was on Lucas' back, biting and clawing with all she had in her.

Slocum grabbed Lucy and threw her off the cliff, following her a second later. The gun fired twice as they fell.

The shock of hitting the cold, churning seawater was paralyzing. Slocum plunged underwater and his mind froze; he completely forgot to do anything but sink. A strong sense of *déjà vu* was the first awareness that permeated his consciousness. He remembered his underwater dream of two days ago and the memory jump-started him. It finally dawned on Slocum that Lucy was nearby and was probably scared out of her mind. He kicked his freezing legs frantically and managed to surface. Sirens wailed close by — that was good — but he couldn't see Lucy anywhere — that was very bad. A second later, she broke into the air, gasping and spluttering. She was about twelve feet away from Slocum, but the current was already dragging her towards the rocks.

"Can you swim?" Slocum shouted.

"What?"

"Can you swim?"

"This is a hell of a time to ask me that!" she called back. "But yes--I can!"

"Great!"

The sea lions decided to bark replies to this exchange, making further communication problematical.

"Turn around!" Slocum directed.

"What?"

"Turn around!"

"What?"

"Behind you!" He managed to point as he yelled this time.

Lucy swivelled her head just as the boat reached her. Greg unceremoniously hauled her in by the arms and headed for Slocum. In his black wetsuit, in the dark, their rescuer looked like a sea lion himself.

The small wooden launch arrived in the nick of time. Weighed down by his wet clothes, his strength sapped by the cold water, Slocum could barely tread water by the time Greg maneuvered close enough to grab him by the shoulders.

The air felt even colder than the ocean, and the interaction of the salt water and air on Slocum's cuts and scratches provided its share of agony as well. He clutched Lucy and they huddled under several blankets.

"I thought you guys were goners," Greg told them.

"Me too," Lucy agreed, her teeth chattering.

A searchlight flashed across them and returned to impale them with its impossibly bright beam.

"This is the police," a bullhorned voice told them. "Stay where you are. A police cruiser will be there shortly to pick you up. If you try to leave, we'll shoot."

"You got it, chief!" Greg called back.

"Could you hear Flinch call to you?" Slocum asked.

"From up there? Hell no."

"Then they can't hear you either. Just don't drive away."

"You don't drive in a boat."

"Whatever."

Lucy began sobbing in Slocum's arms. She was crying so hard she could barely breathe. As he pulled her closer, he spoke soothingly. "It's all right. We're all right now."

"So what happened?" Greg asked.

Slocum alternated between filling him in and comforting Lucy as they waited for the police. For once, Greg's response was completely devoid of humor.

"My God," was his only comment.

Twenty-Seven

After many hours of individual interrogation, confusion, discomfort, sleep deprivation, and general wretchedness, Detective Perry reunited the threesome in his office. The black man stood behind his desk chair, leaning on it with stiffly extended arms. His face, body language, and filthy wrinkled clothes reflected the hour. It was five a.m.

Greg, Slocum and Lucy were arrayed in that order on folding wooden chairs across the desk from Perry. Slocum and Lucy wore orange jail jumpsuits, which had been supplied in lieu of their soggy clothes. Greg was still in his black wetsuit. Even with all the zippers open as far as decency permitted, he was still sweating like a pig inside it. His unkempt beard was actually dripping.

The office was a singularly boring room, displaying no personalized details beyond the institutional necessities. The desk was old, scarred, and wooden, although somebody had recently grafted white formica onto the top of it. A black phone and various piles of papers covered most of the shiny surface. There were no wall decorations, and it was still too dark outside to make out whatever view was ordinarily available through the one window.

"Don't you have any family?" Greg asked, gesturing vaguely with a rubber-covered arm. "I thought cops kept pictures of their families in their offices."

"Shut up," Perry answered in a genial tone of voice.

"We're in the clear," Slocum told the others. "He's ruthlessly polite when he's breathing down your neck."

Perry smiled wanly. "That's right. Morino's the bad cop."

"Where is Mr. Charm anyway?" Greg asked.

"He headed over to the hospital with the chief of police, the sheriff, and a crew of detectives. At this point, that's where the action is." He navigated around the chair, sat down, and propped his head up on a fist. Perry's eyes were bloodshot, especially in the corners nearest the bridge of his wide, flat nose. He badly needed a shave too — his beard was nearly as fast-growing as Slocum's. "I appreciate your patience," he told the threesome. "You're free to go at this point, but I figured you'd want to be apprised of what we know before you left."

"How's the dog?" Lucy asked.

"She'll live. They've been pulling pellets out of her all night at the emergency vet's. She got the best of Mr. Beecham in their final exchange."

"He didn't shoot her?" Slocum asked.

"No. He tried, but you should see his back. The man has vertebrate showing. Nobody in the emergency room had ever seen anything like it. That's no ordinary dog."

"What about Feng Shi? How's he doing?" Lucy asked.

"He's still in serious condition at Dominican Hospital, but at least he's out of intensive care. Apparently he took a shotgun blast to the shoulder and then a nine millimeter hollow point to the same shoulder later. He can forget about that shoulder — even with reconstructive work it's never going to be functional — but the rest of him ought to be okay. He was able to give a statement, by the way, which is the main reason you three are in the clear. Beecham told him quite a bit while you were listening to the doctored tape."

"Why was he even there?" Greg asked. "I mean Shi knew *he* wasn't the killer, so he must've figured Lucas was, but then he shows up and stands around jawing with the guy. I don't get it."

"It was another elaborate con," Perry explained, "planned and executed carefully over the last few months. It's too complicated for someone as tired as me to explain right now, but it involved esoteric spiritual knowledge — something about dreams and energy that their teacher was involved in. Hell, even if I was alert I probably couldn't explain it. But it worked on Feng Shi — that's what matters."

"What did the doctors say about him?" Slocum asked.

"He's the healthiest elderly man they've ever seen. I'm told he has the musculature of an active fifty-year-old."

"How about Flinch?" Greg asked. "He got shot in the leg, right?"

"The thigh, actually. He lost a lot of blood — more than any of the others — but he'll live too. That is, if the nursing staff doesn't kill him." Perry smiled.

"I should've just called for Flinch in the first place instead of screwing around with the empty shotgun," Slocum confessed. "It feels pretty weird to be sitting here intact while everyone else is off bleeding somewhere. I mean I was the one making the mistakes, but they're the ones paying the price."

"Hey," Lucy said, turning to face Slocum. "If it weren't for you, we'd all be dead. And everybody isn't off bleeding. There's the three of us here that are doing just fine."

"My whole plan was stupid," Slocum replied gloomily. "We could easily have killed ourselves going off the cliff, and Flinch's hole was totally in the wrong place."

"You were lucky to get out in one piece," Perry replied. "I'll grant you that. But from my perspective, where you went wrong was way before tonight." He straightened his posture and spoke in a sterner voice. "You know, if you'd been straight with me two days ago, all of this could've been avoided."

"You're right," Slocum responded. "I'm sorry!"

"But I would've missed out on all the fun!" Greg interrupted enthusiastically.

Everyone stared at him; Perry sighed and lowered his head back onto his propped arm.

"Any more questions?" he asked wearily.

"Well, what's the deal with Lucas? Have you got a good case against him?" Lucy asked.

"We do. He's under arrest on three counts of first degree murder and about ten other things. I doubt if our staff psychiatrist has ever seen anything like him either. I know I haven't. He's brilliant, charismatic, and terrifyingly convincing. He's also psychotic and completely amoral — a policeman's worst nightmare.

"Basically, though, his motivation was greed, like anyone else who doesn't kill in a fit of passion. Brahmachari willed his holdings, which are considerable, to whichever of his lieutenants was ultimately the sole survivor. The assets have been in trust for years. It's something you don't do if you're a Mafia chieftain, but I imagine the guy felt it was a safe bet with these people." Perry shifted his weight and leaned back in his chair. He seemed more alert than he'd been earlier. "Beecham had cooked up a double frame. First he nailed Slocum here, which was a little too perfect to satisfy me. I mean who puts the murder weapon under his living room chair and then invites the police in to look around? But Beecham had that figured. While Slocum was in jail, he was going to take out Rinpoche Tilopa, which got him off the hook, but was designed to frame Feng Shi. That way Shi looks like he was framing Slocum. Finally, there was going to be a showdown between Beecham and Shi in which Beecham had to defend himself with his pistol — end of suspect, case closed."

"So Slocum's escaping wrecked his plan?" Greg asked.

"Complicated it," the detective replied. "Now he had more loose ends to tie up in his showdown scenario. I tell you, I think the guy has watched too many westerns. Anyway, if you guys had been just a little bit dumber, Beecham would've walked away, and all the physical evidence would've indicated that you'd killed each other out at the lighthouse. He had a very well thought out plan."

"Except for Karma," Greg said.

"Well I wouldn't know about that," Perry responded. "I'll leave the philosophy to you young folks."

"Karma is the dog's name." Lucy told him.

"Oh. Sorry. I knew that — I'm just a little too beat to do this right." He lowered his head again and massaged his temples. "Anything else?" he asked.

Slocum was asleep in his chair and had been for some time.

"Who's going to drive us home?" Lucy asked.

Marc Darrow, currently a psychotherapist in Santa Cruz, California, has pursued a variety of careers, including professional volleyball player in Italy, import store owner, country-western singer/songwriter, university coach/P.E. instructor, and assistant guru. Marc is married, loves dogs, and welcomes correspondence.

Mystery in the Monterey Bay Area Series

The Santa Cruz Guru Murders — Marc Darrow
Shrinking The Truth — Marc Darrow
Hole in the Heart — Mark Mosca

The following Patrick Riordan mysteries, written by
Roy Gilligan, also take place in the Monterey Bay Area:

Chinese Restaurants Never Serve Breakfast
Live Oaks Also Die
Poets Never Kill
Happiness Is Often Deadly
Playing God... and Other Games
Just Another Murder in Miami
Dead Heat from Big Sur
Stab in the Bach

Novels with Monterey Bay Area locations:

Green Bananas — Michael Drinkard
A Much-Married Man - Robert Sward
Gig — James D. Houston
Gasoline — James D. Houston
Mordecai of Monterey — Keith Abbott